D1395562

Gabe's mouth covered Elly's without a hint of hesitation. He knew exactly where to go and what to do to make her his.

'Daddy!'

Gabe stiffened and instantly broke the kiss. Shock scarred his handsome face, giving it a haggardness she'd never seen before, and her blood turned to ice. 'What's wrong, Gabe? What's happened?'

'Daddy!'

A toddler threw himself at Gabe, who hastily rose to his feet, swinging the child up into his arms. 'Hey, honey-pie.'

Daddy? Honey-pie?

Elly stared at the blonde little girl whose head rested so trustingly against Gabe's chest. 'You…have a child?'

Elly swung around to see two identical dark-haired little boys, making a bee-line for Gabe. She swayed as the world started to spin. Gabe had three children all under two.

Triplets!

Always an avid reader, **Fiona Lowe** decided to combine her love of romance with her interest in all things medical, so writing Medical™ Romance was an obvious choice! She lives in a seaside town in southern Australia, where she juggles writing, reading, working and raising two gorgeous sons with the support of her own real-life hero!

Recent books by the same author:

THE MOST MAGICAL GIFT OF ALL
HER BROODING HEART SURGEON
MIRACLE: TWIN BABIES

SINGLE DAD'S TRIPLE TROUBLE

BY
FIONA LOWE

All the characters in this book have no existence outside
the imagination of the author, and have no relation
whatsoever to anyone bearing the same name or names.
They are not even distantly inspired by any individual
known or unknown to the author, and all the incidents
are pure invention.

All Rights Reserved including the right of reproduction
in whole or in part in any form. This edition is published
by arrangement with Harlequin Enterprises II BV/S.à.r.l.
The text of this publication or any part thereof may
not be reproduced or transmitted in any form or by
any means, electronic or mechanical, including
photocopying, recording, storage in an information
retrieval system, or otherwise, without the written
permission of the publisher.

® and TM are trademarks owned and used by the
trademark owner and/or its licensee. Trademarks marked
with ® are registered with the United Kingdom Patent
Office and/or the Office for Harmonisation in the
Internal Market and in other countries.

First published in Great Britain 2011
by Mills & Boon,
an imprint of Harlequin (UK) Limited,
Large Print edition 2011
Eton House, 18-24 Paradise Road,
Richmond, Surrey TW9 1SR

© Fiona Lowe 2011

ISBN: 978 0 263 21757 5

Harlequin (UK) policy is to use papers that are
natural, renewable and recyclable products and made
from wood grown in sustainable forests. The logging
and manufacturing process conform to the legal
environmental regulations of the country of origin.

Printed and bound in Great Britain
by CPI Antony Rowe, Chippenham, Wiltshire

SINGLE DAD'S TRIPLE TROUBLE

To Meg.
We've travelled together for twelve books
and the journey continues to be a pleasure.
Thanks for your sage advice and support.

CHAPTER ONE

'I CAN'T believe I'm actually saying this, but I don't think he's the one for you.'

Elly Ruddock, GP, community member of Coast-Care, and desperately late for the annual 'blessing of the fleet' dinner, spritzed perfume on her wrists, slid an emerald-green bead necklace around her throat and tried unsuccessfully to block out the conversation she'd had earlier in the day with her friend, Sarah.

'Dev is a good man.' Elly had defended her date for the evening. 'Besides, you're the one who sat me down two months ago, called me a "one-date wonder" and said I'd sabotaged every attempt at a relationship since I'd arrived.' She'd over-stirred her latte as indignation had partnered up with disquiet. 'Besides, this is my fifth date with Dev and now you're telling me he's not right. You can't have it both ways, Sarah.'

The nurse and mother had rescued her keys from her toddler and sighed. 'Just be careful you're not confusing good and solid with dull and boring.'

Thankfully Elly's mobile phone had rung at that exact moment, ending the conversation, and she'd rushed to the hospital to treat a child who'd been knocked off his bike by a car. The emergency had consumed the rest of the afternoon and was the reason she was now so late for the dinner.

She threw lipstick and her phone into an evening bag and snapped it shut. Dev Johnston was *not* boring. He was CEO of the shire, reliable, dependable, coached the under-twelves' cricket team and, most importantly, he was unlikely to break her heart.

'I love you, El, but I can't give you what you want.'

She tugged on her wardrobe door and rummaged through her evening shoes, most of them rarely worn these days because Midden Cove's night life didn't come within a bull's roar of Melbourne. When she'd told her friends and family she was relocating to the verdant island of Tasmania, she'd dealt with raised brows and knowing looks. Her mother had accused her of running away. Her sister, Suzy, who was happily married with twin daughters, had said, 'Hobart isn't Sydney, sis,' which was code for the dating pool being small. There was an element of truth in both statements.

But when they'd found out she was bypassing Hobart completely and going to an isolated coastal hamlet, they'd threatened therapy. She'd retaliated by saying that good men, men who wanted the same things out of life as she did, turned up in unlikely places. At least she'd know straight up that living in a country town would be something both she and a future partner wanted.

So far, after two years in Midden Cove, she'd met a lot of good men. Most of them married, many of them grandfathers, and far too many were her patients. That left the guys who came to town and worked the season in the tourist industry, the principal of the primary school and the shire employees. She'd dated them all and Dev was the last eligible bachelor left in the district.

The old grandfather clock chimed seven and the doorbell pealed. Unlike her, Dev was never late. She grabbed her shoes and ran.

Dr Gabe Lewis stroked the heads of his sleeping children and found it hard to believe that whirling tornadoes could look this angelic in sleep. He stifled a yawn, his body wanting to fall into bed with them and crash into a deep and uninterrupted sleep; a sleep he hadn't known for well over a year.

'Gabe, you'll be late if you don't leave now.' His mother spoke quietly from the doorway. 'Dad and I have got everything under control.'

I wish I did. 'Thanks, Mum.' He really didn't want to go to the yacht club but his parents thought they were helping by giving him a night off and he didn't have the heart to disappoint them. His reputation as the party guy had taken such a severe battering in the last eighteen months that he hardly recognised himself. 'Ring me if you need me.'

'I raised you, your brother and sister, and I'm sure I can handle your three for a night.' Concern was etched deeply around her eyes. 'Visiting us is supposed to be a holiday for you as well as the kids. Go out and have some fun, Gabe. You need it.'

Fun. He'd forgotten the concept.

The speeches were over, dessert had been eaten and the band swung into a retro set. The music filled Elly's veins and her feet tapped under the table but Dev didn't move from his chair. He was totally engrossed in outlining his plans for the foreshore conservation project and the protection of the fairy penguin colony. It wasn't that she wasn't interested, she was, but he'd spoken about it in such detail that she knew more about the programme than the workers who'd be implementing it.

He suddenly gave a self-conscious laugh. 'I'm boring you.'

She shook her head, almost too quickly. 'It's wonderful that you're so passionate about your job.'

Leaning forward, he picked up her hand. 'You look lovely tonight, Eleanor.'

She smiled, pushing down deep the fact that she'd asked him to call her Elly at least five times. 'Thank you.'

'I really enjoy spending time with you.'

'So do I.' *Mostly.*

'We share a lot of things in common and five dates is a bit of a watershed, don't you think?' His serious brown eyes roved over her face. 'I want to spend a *lot* more time with you.'

The noise of the room seeped away, deafened by the pounding of blood in her head. A lot more time meant a serious relationship. A chance at a family?

'I don't want children, El, it's just not me.'

Dev cleared his throat. 'I'm not rushing you, Eleanor, but I need you to understand that I'm looking for a relationship that's going to move forward into the future. One for the long haul with a view to marriage, kids and a superannuation portfolio. We can go slowly, but if what I've just said isn't something you can see in your future then let me down now.'

'You've sabotaged every relationship in twenty-three months.'

His fingers stroked hers but only a slight shimmer of warmth wove through her, like weak sunshine on a cold day.

Without warning, vivid recollections from the past thundered in, mocking her tepid response. Memories of molten lust pounded her, reminding her how need had once poured through her so strong and fast that she'd been incapable of standing, and that long desire-fuelled days had been spent in tangled sheets. But all of that wonder had ended with her heart being shattered.

'Sexual attraction is overrated. Dev's a good man, you share things in common, and you both want children.'

She bit her lip, pushed her past down deep and squeezed his hand. 'I want to try.'

He shot to his feet, dropped a perfunctory kiss onto her forehead and twirled her out onto the dance floor. The tiny parquet floor was crowded as everyone rocked and jived, dancing in a communal group rather than as intimate couples.

Dev laughed as he spun away from her, joining

in an impromptu twist competition. Elly smiled, watching the dancers strut their stuff, and reminded herself that this was what living in a small community was all about. Sharing. After all, it wasn't like Dev had just proposed to her, but that didn't stop disappointment from niggling that he wasn't dancing with her cheek to cheek as a sign that something significant had just happened between them.

'We've had a request from the commodore for the barn dance.' Joel Rubens—the grandson of the commodore—whose spiked black hair and body piercings made him look like he'd be more at home playing punk rock than parlour music—obviously knew that payment came only if he did as he was asked. 'So can all the ladies make a circle and then you blokes go stand next to the woman you came with.' He leaned into the microphone and winked. 'Of course, you might not get to go home with her after this raunchy dance.'

Elly stepped into the circle and Dev found her, sliding his arm lightly around her waist as the traditional folk music started up. She stepped in closer, fighting the feeling she was dancing with her brother.

Dev tightened his arm around her and smiled as he expertly executed the steps to the dance. 'Enjoy yourself,' he said, and he danced her into the arms of the next man.

As she danced around the room, she danced with the mayor and with schoolboys who loved to sail, she danced with shopkeepers and wood turners, sawmill owners, hobby farmers and fishermen—the eclectic and caring community of Midden Cove; her adopted town and one she loved. Her feet were taking a pounding as not all Midden Cove men had smooth moves but she forgave them as the sense of belonging washed over her. The burly woodcutter thanked her for caring for his mother recently and then twirled her on.

Strong, tanned arms, with a smattering of golden hair enveloped her, as did the scent of musk, soap and danger. Her head jerked up and suddenly she was looking into the bluest-of-blue eyes that sparkled like the facets of a sapphire. Eyes she knew. Eyes that had dazzled her before and had once flickered with undiluted lust just for her.

Her breath turned solid in her chest, all words sticking in her throat, and her feet stumbled, pushing her against his broad and muscular chest. A chest whose every convex and concave line was tattooed on her brain for ever. It only took one brief touch of his hand and her body lit up like the fireworks-filled-sky on New Year's Eve.

Long fingers laced through hers, pulling her arm up in a perfect dance square. His other arm gripped her waist, holding her upright as her legs melted. 'Deep breath, El. It's just one dance and it'll soon be over.'

And less than five steps later she'd been spun out to her next partner. Somehow she managed to finish the barn dance and join in with the enthusiastic clapping at the end. But as Dev's hand reached for hers, her eyes strayed across the room to the bar, taking in very familiar sun-bleached hair, and broad, dress-shirt-clad shoulders. Her head spun, making silver spots dance before her eyes. What was adventure-seeking, high-living Gabe Lewis doing in tiny Midden Cove?

Elly's heart hammered so hard she was sure everyone could hear it. As the band took a break, people drifted off to the bar and out onto the deck, and she excused herself, dashing to the ladies.

Deep breath, El.

She gulped air into her cramping lungs. Gabe had always been the calm one. Calm, laid back and easygoing, unless crossed. When people hit his stubborn streak for the first time, it always led to shocked surprise. She should have heeded the warning the first time their opinions had differed.

Her breathing almost steadied as she gave herself a stern talking to. What did it matter that Gabe was in town? It didn't matter at all. Sure, they shared a past but that's exactly what it was: history. They'd broken up almost two years ago, their relationship floundering on the rocks of irreconcilable differences.

She raised her eyes to the mirror and groaned at her pale image. How could she be so rattled by seeing him again when he'd looked so composed and at ease? Damn it, she'd spent months getting over him and she was furious with herself for turning into a quivering mess at one brief touch. She stiffened her spine. She was over him. She *had* to be over him. With trembling fingers, she smoothed down her hair. This reaction was just the unexpected shock of seeing him again after all this time and the next time she saw him she'd be just as cool as he'd been.

You go, girl. She opened her evening bag, wound out her lipstick and swiped cherry red across her lips; ignoring the fact it was the only colour on her face.

Women drifted in and out of the bathroom, smiling and chatting, and Elly knew she couldn't stay locked away much longer. She took one last glance in the mirror, tilted her chin and pushed open the door.

Joel had the microphone in his hand and was nodding to the bass guitarist, who was plugging in his guitar. 'We're going to play you a song we wrote so stand by as we rock this room.'

The screeching noise of feedback squealed through the amplifiers and the guitarist put down his instrument and adjusted the sound. 'Sorry, guys, we're just gonna change amps.'

Elly started to move across the crowded room toward the deck, thinking that the best place to hear an original Fires' composition was as far away from the amplifiers as possible. As she reached the halfway point, the lights suddenly flickered then almost simultaneously a deafening bang ricocheted around the room. An arc of silver-white light flared and the room was plunged into darkness as a stomach-curdling, piercing yelp rent the air.

'Doc Elly!' Joel screamed in terror.

Elly swung round and helpful hands pushed her forward, as she used the moonlight to find her way. Just as she reached the stage a hand gripped her upper arm and tugged her back.

A smooth, deep voice spoke firmly but quietly in her ear.

'Wait. I don't want you fried too.' With his fingers still pressing into the soft flesh of her arm, Gabe called out in a commanding tone, 'Has the power been turned off?'

'Yes.' The barman held up a torch providing much-needed light.

'Are you absolutely certain?'

He gave a brisk nod. 'I did it myself.'

'Go.' Gabe's arm fell from Elly's.

She pulled her dress up above her knees before clambering onto the stage. As her eyes searched in the dim light around all the sound equipment and musical instruments, she heard Gabe announcing he was a doctor and instructing someone to get his medical bag from his car. She bumped into the drum kit, the cymbals clashing loudly, and then she saw Joel crouching down over the inert body of the guitarist.

'Will plugged in the amp and…and then he flew backwards.' Joel's shadowed eyes reflected the horror of watching his mate being electrocuted.

'Gabe, call an ambulance!' She rushed forward, her fingers reaching for the unconscious man's carotid pulse. She felt around. Nothing.

'Mate.' Gabe's firm step sounded on the stage and he touched Joel on the shoulder.

Joel stared at him blankly.

Gabe spoke slowly. 'Go to the front of the yacht

club and meet the ambulance so you can bring them straight to us, OK?'

'Will he be OK?'

'We're doing our best.' Elly checked her patient's mouth for any obstruction and then with her fingers under his chin she tilted his head back.

'You breathe, I'll compress.' Gabe knelt beside her, his expression wry. 'Just like old times, El.'

'Only without the back-up of a state-of-the-art hospital.' She knew she sounded brusque but she didn't want to think of old times spent at work, and no way was she thinking about old times spent together away from work. That had jeopardy written all over it.

Like a well-oiled machine they fell into the emergency, each of them anticipating the other, seamlessly working toward the same wished-for outcome.

'Still no pulse. We need the ambulance and the lifepack.'

'We need more light—and where's my medical kit?' Gabe's muscular arms pushed against Will's chest, compressing blood through the heart and urging it to start pumping again.

'Emergency lights are on their way but we've got five torches.' The barman slid Gabe's medical kit onto the stage and organised Dev and three other men to hold torches above them.

'On my count, El, you start compressing and I'll attach him to the AED.'

Surprise competed with relief. 'You travel with an automated external defibrillator?'

He shrugged. 'Once an emergency specialist, always one.'

With expert fingers, he connected Will to the tiny but rugged lifesaving device. 'All clear.'

Elly kneeled back, making sure no part of her was touching Will. 'Clear.'

Gabe discharged the AED but the heart rate traced across the screen like a squiggly line. His normally wide and smiling mouth flattened grimly. 'He's in ventricular fibrillation.'

Elly resumed compressions and Gabe prepared to shock again.

'All clear.'

Will bucked as the electricity shot through his body but the longed-for change didn't occur.

'Adrenaline.' Elly kept up the cardiopulmonary resuscitation, shutting out how good it felt to be working with Gabe again.

'On it.' He quickly tore open a large bore butterfly cannula pack, and with the skill born of years of practice he slid it into the large vein on the inner aspect of Will's arm. He immediately followed with the adrenaline. 'Come on, Will.'

'Let it work this time.' Elly bit her lip as she kneeled back.

'God knows what's burned inside him.'

The quiet words mirrored her thoughts. They might get Will's heart beating properly but the hidden damage might be just as life-threatening.

'All clear.' Gabe's fingers pressed the button.

Time rolled out at one-eighth speed as both of them stared at the visual display, willing it to show a normal heartbeat.

'Yes! Sinus rhythm.' Elly grinned at Gabe, high on the buzz of teamwork and a good save.

He met her gaze, his eyes sparkling with his

own high, and her heart took a shock. Heat scudded through her and like oxygen to a flame it sparked and fanned the deeply buried ashes of her longing. Shimmers of delicious need tingled along her veins, diving deep until the embers flared into a hot and raging fire. Her hands trembled on the air-viva. *Look away now!* She dropped her gaze and concentrated on puffing air into Will's lungs.

'I need ice in towels for his burns,' Gabe yelled to the torch bearers, the sound slightly strangled.

They continued to work in silence until the paramedics arrived and Elly gave a handover. 'We're taking him to the hospital's helipad because he needs to be airlifted to Hobart, but I'll ride with the ambulance.'

Gabe stood up. 'I'll call the Royal and meet you at the hospital.'

Dev stepped up. 'Eleanor, ring me from the hospital when you're ready to go home.'

She swung round. God, she'd forgotten all about Dev and the fact he'd driven her to the yacht club. 'I could be hours, Dev.'

Gabe's shoulders rolled back and he clapped Dev on the shoulder. 'Don't worry, mate, I'll make sure she gets home safely.'

For the first time Dev's eyes narrowed. 'And exactly who are you?'

Gabe extended his hand. 'Gabe Lewis, doctor, and good friend of Elly's.'

Friends? Snapshot images of their time together formed a montage in her mind—lovers, colleagues and combatants were words that came instantly to mind, but friends? Perhaps once, but not now. Not when he'd broken her heart so badly.

'Ready when you are, Doc.'

The senior paramedic brought her back to the moment and she nodded, checking Will's vital signs. 'Let's go.' With the air-viva in her hand she walked out, steeling herself not to look back.

CHAPTER TWO

'So, what's a girl like you doing in a tiny joint like this?'

The moment the roar of the helicopter blades had receded to a distant buzz, Gabe asked the question that had been constantly playing in his head from the second he'd spotted Elly at the yacht club. He hadn't expected to meet anyone he knew from Melbourne, or from anywhere else for that matter, let alone Elly. He'd seen her across the room five minutes before she'd danced into his arms, giving him a few precious minutes to dig deep and attempt to cover his stunned and shocked surprise.

God, she looked amazing. Different, but still amazing. When his arms had wrapped around her soft, lush curves and when he'd breathed in her tantalising scent of tropical fruit and the tang of the ocean, he'd experienced the completely unexpected sensation of not wanting to let her go. But he knew that was just the trickery of memory and the body's craving for familiar things. They'd split two years ago, with Elly accusing him of letting her leave and him furious that she wouldn't stay. Now so much had changed in his life that craving for the past was pointless.

Craving for any woman was pointless because after what he'd been through with Jenna he was keeping his very complicated life as simple as possible. Work and the children consumed every waking hour and a good part of the night, and he had no energy left for anything else.

Her dainty sandals clacked against the gravel as they walked toward the hospital. 'I live here, Gabe. You might recall that moving out of the inner city was something I talked about.' Emerald-green eyes hit him with a bone-weary look. 'It wasn't something that you wanted so it makes more sense for me to be the one asking what a guy like you is doing in a tiny town like Midden Cove. I thought your plan included trekking in Nepal and base jumping in Norway.'

He recognised the hurt in her eyes, hurt he'd

help put there and she'd cemented in. 'I did the base jump but I haven't got to Nepal.'

Her chestnut brows rose. 'You've had two years, Gabe. What have you been doing? It's not like you to let the grass grow under your feet.'

Jenna's blank face swam before his eyes and he had to work hard not to flinch. *Just keep it light.*

'Oh, you know me, I go with the flow and it hasn't taken me to Nepal yet, but one day it will.' Knowing that in the past Elly had often lost her train of thought when he'd smiled at her, he gave her a full-wattage beam in a desperate attempt to derail her.

She didn't even blink. 'But the flow has brought you here?'

Hell, this was going to be harder than he'd thought. He refused to talk about the real reason he was in Midden Cove, not yet anyway, but he knew he had to give her something so the questions would stop. 'There's great sea kayaking around the peninsula.'

'Isn't that a bit tame compared with base jumping?' Her usually open and friendly demeanour had a distinct chill.

He opened the door to A and E and forced himself to lean back as she passed through before him. 'Not when there's a sou-wester blowing. But mostly I'm in town because my parents recently retired down here and I'm visiting them.'

'James and Cathleen Lewis are your parents?'

Her eyes widened to rippling pools of green that called to him, tempting him to dive in deep and become part of her. *You moron. Haven't you learned anything in two years? Desire like this will only cause you more heartache.*

A barbed arrow of reality plunged in deeply. *Hell, she knew his parents!* He silently dammed small towns and hoped against hope his mother hadn't shown Elly her wallet photos of the children. 'Yep, that's Mum and Dad.' He worked on keeping his tone casual. 'Are they patients of yours?'

She shook her head, her knuckles whitening on the edges of her white coat. 'No, but if they need medical care in the next few weeks then they'll see me as I'm the only doctor in town at the moment. I've met them briefly at a Coast-Care meeting but I didn't make the connection with you.'

A breath of relief rushed out. He wanted to be the person who told her about the children. He owed her that but blurting it out on their first meeting wasn't the way to go. 'There's no reason for you to connect them with me. As you say, me and small towns are not exactly a match, and when we were dating they were living in Hong Kong.' Words tumbled over each other and he worked on slowing them down to his usual laid-back speed. 'Dad's decided he wants to be sur-rounded by vast tracks of space. I give him a year and he'll be chomping at the bit to head back to the mainland.'

'You might be surprised. Midden Cove has a way of getting into your blood.' She tucked her chin-length hair behind her ear.

A snag of something akin to disappointment slugged him. He'd always loved her long, soft locks. Loved burying his face and hands in their silky length and breathing in their rich vanilla scent. 'You changed your hair.'

The corner of her mouth lifted, the action re-signed. 'I changed a lot of things, Gabe. Some changes were forced on me and some I chose myself.'

Old hurt rumbled through him at her choice to leave him. Almost two years ago they'd both been immovable about what they wanted and unfortunately those wants had been poles apart. 'Fair enough.'

She scrawled her signature across Will's paper-work and then slipped off her white coat, expos-ing lightly tanned shoulders.

His gaze immediately drifted lower to the bead-adorned neckline and the hint of creamy soft breasts that nestled underneath. Breasts he'd once considered his. Blood pounded directly to his groin as memories of long afternoons spent ex-ploring every centimetre of her body rushed back with an intensity that shocked him. His libido had been AWOL for months and this was a seriously inconvenient time for it to return.

Picking up her evening bag, she spoke brusquely. 'You can drop me home now.'

He stifled a groan and tried to pull his recalcitrant body back together. The offer to drive her home had been spontaneously made the moment he'd laid eyes on the up-tight bloke who'd called her Eleanor. Now, the idea of sitting in the close confines of his car with Elly seemed too much like a temptation he'd have to work hard to resist. 'Sure. Let's go.'

He fished his keys out of his pocket and they walked silently into the now-inky night. He looked up and stopped. The Southern Cross hung low, and the Milky Way wove through the sky like a carpet of dazzling crystals. 'This sky is amazing.'

Elly shrugged as if it was no big deal. 'The moonshine's masking most of it but if you hang around long enough it will fade and you might even see the aurora australis.'

'The southern lights? You can see them from here?'

'Sure. Midden Cove is one of the best places.'

She left him staring at the sky and opened the car door, settling herself in the passenger seat.

His body went rigid and he starting walking again, this time very quickly. Hell, how had he forgotten about the car? He hauled open his door, thankful he'd turned out the interior light after too many flat batteries, and hoped she wouldn't glance into the back seat where the moonlight silhouetted the children's car seats.

He slid into the leather seat and pressed the ignition button. 'So where's your place?' Perhaps she'd invite him in and then he'd tell her about the children.

'Turn right and take the second left.' The metal of her seat belt clanged against the plastic lock as she tried to find the clasp.

'Here, let me.' He leaned over and her hair brushed his cheek as he snapped the buckle into place. The infusion of berries and the beach filled his nostrils and he hated the way he found himself breathing more deeply.

'I can't believe you parted with the Porsche.'

He felt her intense gaze on him as he steered the vehicle out of the car park. 'It's tucked up in

the garage in South Yarra. This four-wheel drive
is good for getting up to the out-of-the-way places
for hang gliding.' *True, but it's not the reason
you bought it.*

She glanced at the BMW logo. 'I think the
locals would call this a Toorak truck, not a four-
wheel drive.'

He rolled his eyes. 'I'll make sure I get it dirty
so it can hold its own in the car park.'

She laughed, a throaty, joyous sound devoid of
all the tension that had been rolling off her from
the moment she'd looked up into his eyes at the
dance. 'My place is just up here on the left with
the ti-tree hedge.'

He slowed, his headlights making out the hedge
and catching glimpses of what looked like an
old fishing cottage; the antithesis of the spacious
apartment they'd shared in Melbourne. Once,
they'd shared a lot of things.

She clicked the release on her seat belt, her tension slotting back into place like a wall. 'Thanks
for dropping me home and I hope you have a
lovely visit with your parents.'

No hint of an invitation there, pal. Well, hell,

he could match her strained politeness and raise it. 'It's great to see you. Perhaps we can have coffee and catch up at a more sensible time?' *So I can tell you about the children.*

'I don't think so, Gabe.'

This time the barb stung and he snapped. 'Look, I'm being polite here in a difficult situation. I had no clue you'd moved to Midden Cove. Hell, I didn't even know you'd left Melbourne, so me being here is not in any way part of an attempt at reconciliation.'

Her body recoiled against the seat as if he'd slapped her. 'Lucky I wasn't under any illusions, then, wasn't it.'

Remorse raised its head and he ran his hand through his hair, regretting that he'd inadvertently hurt her. Again. 'I'm sorry, that came out wrong. I get it that you don't want to see me and if you want, I won't bother you while I'm here.'

That means you have to tell her now.

No way, not now, not like this.

Elly gave him a curt nod as her hand reached for the doorhandle, antipathy mingling with her intoxicating scent.

Memories instantly piled up of happier times—moments when they'd laughed until their sides had ached, occasions when they'd finished each other's sentences. Times so far removed from this where they now sat side by side like strangers.

Despite what she'd said about wanting to leave Melbourne, he'd never understood that to mean coming to such an isolated spot as Midden Cove. He gave her a wry smile, and asked the question that had been on his mind from the moment he'd seen her. 'Just tell me one thing. Are you really happy here, El?'

This time she blinked. Twice. Then with a toss of her head, which sent her rich chocolate hair flying around her face, she stepped out of the car. 'I'm perfectly happy, thank you.' Without looking back, she slammed the door shut behind her.

He didn't believe her.

Elly sat at her kitchen table and stared out through her glass patio doors, watching a little blue wren take on his reflection in a territorial battle. That settled it: housework was a health hazard to birds and she shouldn't bother to clean the glass again.

She sipped her tea and tried to focus on what she had to do on this sunny Sunday. Her list was long and she really should get going on it, but her brain was stuck on Gabe.

Gabe was in town.

It shouldn't matter a jot to her that he was in 'the Cove', but her brain mocked her by spinning that one thought around like a scratched CD.

More importantly, how long is he in town? She lowered her mug and groaned. Why hadn't she asked him that last night? But she knew the answer—she'd been petrified that if she did ask she'd sound too desperate. Desperate for him to leave or desperate for him to stay, she wasn't certain, and both ideas had actively competed for a brief moment. So when he'd suggested coffee, she'd panicked and the 'ice queen' had come out to protect her.

Boy, did she need protection. She didn't trust herself not to go down the self-destructive path of wanting to spend time with him, which was completely ironic given his response.

Me being here is not in any way part of an attempt at reconciliation.

Gabe was nothing if not honest. He was right, too. Reconciliation wasn't an option because nothing had changed between them and their lives were on two different trajectories. She took another sip of her tea. She still couldn't believe he hadn't trekked in the Himalayas because it had been the idea of that trip that had precipitated their demise as a couple.

She could remember his excitement clearly as he'd organised the delivery of Nepali food—a meal of dhal with roti and curried vegetables—before making her a cup of chai and presenting it with the glossy brochures. It would have been the third trip they'd taken in a year and it wasn't that she didn't love to travel, she did. But she'd also had an overwhelming need to stop and settle down.

I'm not interested in settling down, El. Come travel the world with me, it will be more fun.

And here she was in Midden Cove, working, and he was still travelling, although not to the places she'd expected.

The past is over, move forward. Giving herself a quick shake, she picked up her phone and got an update on Will, who was still critical and in ICU at Royal Hobart after skin graft surgery to his hands and feet. As she rang off, a text came through from Dev, suggesting lunch. She should go. She started to key in a reply when her phone rang.

'Sorry to call you, Elly, but we've got an elderly tourist here with shortness of breath.' Sandy, the experienced RN, sounded apologetic.

She swallowed a sigh as she glanced at the postcards on her fridge. Her medical practice partner, Jeff, and his family had taken off for a few months' camping around Australia and although she was thrilled they were having such a great trip, the timing for her was lousy. She hadn't had a complete day off in three weeks. 'I'm on my way.'

'How long have you been feeling unwell, Mr McGovern?' Elly's fingers gently probed under her patient's jaw, feeling for raised lymph nodes.

'My name's John, love, and I've had the blasted cold for over a week. It started just as I got off the boat from Melbourne. We've come to visit the grand-kiddies and the new baby, but getting sick has put a bit of a dampener on things.' He sighed. 'Rachel, my daughter, she's not too happy with me now the baby's got the sniffles too.'

Elly felt for the poor bloke. 'Viruses are in the air all the time. So you're Rachel Morgan's dad?'

'That's right.'

Rachel was Jeff's patient so she wasn't really familiar with the family. 'How are you sleeping?'

'That's why I'm here. My cold's pretty much on the turn but it's this damn cough that's really bothering me. The wife's complaining I keep her awake at night.' The grandfather winked at her. 'I thought it prudent not to mention she's snored for years.'

Elly laughed. 'Sounds like a very wise move, John. Did you have a sore throat with this cold?'

'A bit of a sore throat but that's all gone now. I just feel tired, you know, run down.'

She nodded as she picked up a tongue depressor.

'I'll check your throat. Open wide, please.' She peered into the back of his throat, which didn't look inflamed. 'Can you lift up your shirt, please, so I can listen to your chest?'

'Go for your life, Doc.'

Elly pushed her stethoscope into her ears and listened to John's breathing. The lower lobes were clear with no rales, and she ruled out pneumonia. 'You can have a post-viral cough that lingers after a cold.'

John nodded. 'Thing is, this cough seems to be getting worse, not better.'

Elly's radar went on alert. 'How do you mean?'

'Well, when I cough, I can't seem to stop and it's hard to get my breath.'

She checked his pulse, which was regular and ruled out any cardiac issues. 'What about your breathing when you stop coughing?'

'That's fine.'

'Do you or have you ever suffered from asthma?'

He shook his head and gave a tired smile. 'They say Tassie's got the cleanest air in the country but here I am hacking away like I'm a packet-a-day smoker.'

Her phone buzzed. 'Excuse me for just one minute, John.' She took the call from Sandy, who told her that she had four more people with similar symptoms to John waiting to see her. So much for a quiet Sunday.

Elly dropped the receiver back onto the cradle and returned her attention to John. She couldn't smell any cigarette smoke on him but she asked the question anyway. 'Do you smoke?'

'Cancer sticks?' Again he shook his head and started to cough. 'No way.'

The last words were forced out amid a coughing fit that had John leaning forward, his shoulders hunched as he struggled to get in a breath. When it finally passed he slumped in his chair. 'I tell you, Doc, it's wearing me out.'

Elly rubbed the bridge of her nose. 'How many times a day do you cough like this?'

He scratched his head. 'A couple of times an hour, I reckon.'

She suddenly thought of his baby grandchild and with three clicks brought up the Morgan family's medical history on her computer screen. 'You said the baby had a cold too.'

'Yeah. Told you I'm in the doghouse.'

Elly quickly scanned the date of birth of the baby and calculated the age. Three months. 'Has your daughter come in with you?'

John nodded. 'She drove me.'

Elly reached for the phone. 'Sandy, please send in Rachel.' She had a very strong suspicion that the baby had more than a cold.

'John, have you been out much in Midden Cove while you've been here? To the pub or cafés?'

'The wife and I took a cruise the other day, which was lovely, and most days I've walked down to the pub for a beer. You know, get out from under the wife's feet.'

Elly stifled a groan. John had probably coughed over half the town.

Rachel walked in, cradling her baby, followed by an older woman Elly assumed was John's wife.

'Is there something wrong?' The young mother sat down in the chair Elly had pulled up.

Elly spoke slowly. 'Your dad says the baby's

had a cold so I thought while you were here I could examine her.'

Rachel relaxed. 'Thank you. Yesterday I thought it was just the sniffles but Millie's not feeding very well at all today.'

Elly laid the baby on the examination table. As she unwrapped the bunny rug, the wave of longing for a child of her own slugged her under the ribs in the same way it had done for the last three years.

The child whimpered. 'Has she vomited or had trouble breathing?'

'She keeps pulling off the breast but that's because her nose is blocked, right?'

No. Elly noticed the child's breathing was laboured and her lips were tinged with blue. Millie was one sick baby.

'I'm going to send off some throat swabs from John and Millie and although we won't know definitively until the results are in, I have a strong suspicion that they both have whooping cough.'

A stunned expression froze Rachel's face. 'But that's a kid's disease from a hundred years ago. I thought we'd cured it?'

John sucked in a sharp intake of breath as his wife gasped. 'I thought the cough had to sound like a whoop?'

Elly shook her head in answer to both questions. 'Unfortunately, it's still alive and kicking, and adults and young babies don't tend to have the whooping sound.'

Rachel's eyes widened. 'Oh, God, I thought it was just a cold.'

'I want to admit you and Millie into hospital for observation and treatment.' She wrapped up the baby and handed her back to her mother. 'John, I'm going to give you antibiotics so you're no longer infectious, but I have to ask you to stay in isolation at home for three weeks.'

John's hand immediately touched Rachel's shoulder, his face grey with despair. 'Oh, love, I'm so sorry.'

'It's not your fault, John.' Elly quickly tried to reassure them all. 'Whooping cough has sporadic outbreaks and is always out in the community. It's just unfortunate that Millie's too young to have had all her immunisations. I need to treat everyone in the household and anyone else you've been in close contact with.'

John's wife emitted a wail. 'We were at the christening party on Sunday and we all cuddled the other three babies who were baptised with Millie.'

Elly pulled out a sheet of paper, trying to work out the best way to tackle the fact she had a possible epidemic of whooping cough on her hands. 'OK, I need you to write me a list of everyone you know you've been in close contact with, especially young children and anyone who might not have been immunised against whooping cough.'

Her head raced as she jotted down all the things she had to do, which included notifying the health department and filling in all the paperwork that a communicable disease generated. The phone interrupted her thoughts.

'Elly.' Sandy's usually calm voice sounded stressed. 'Karen Jennings has just arrived with her baby, who's having trouble breathing.'

Elly closed her eyes and breathed deeply. She was just one doctor and she had two sick babies and a growing queue of patients with similar symptoms to John. The babies needed close observation and she needed to treat everyone else as well as set up a vaccination clinic. Help from the health department in Hobart was hours away.

Gabe.

No, there has to be another way.

But she knew that was just wishful thinking. The people of Midden Cove needed another doctor as soon as possible and Gabe fitted that criteria. The fact he was her ex-lover and had pulverised her heart was totally irrelevant.

It had to be.

CHAPTER THREE

'WHOOPING cough?' Gabe quickly absorbed Elly's news, having rushed to the hospital after hearing her tense and stressed voice on the phone. He gave silent thanks that his children were all old enough to have been fully immunised, otherwise he wouldn't have been able to help.

'Yes, whooping cough and at least four babies have been exposed to it.' Elly tucked back the few strands of hair that he was learning always fell forward against her cheek. Hair that his fingers itched to brush back so he could feel the silken strands caressing his skin, just like they had in his dream last night.

From the moment he'd dropped her home from the hospital, he hadn't been able to stop thinking about her. Thinking about them as a couple. They'd been separated now for longer than they'd been together and when they'd parted he'd made the decision not to ever think back. There'd been no point; at first because he'd been too angry and hurt at her uncompromising position and abrupt departure, and then when his life had spiralled so far out of control with Jenna, thinking back and wishing for what might have been with Elly would have been a one-way ticket to despair. Elly hadn't trusted him enough or loved him enough to stay, and Jenna had burned him so badly that the thought of any relationship had him ducking for cover. Yet last night he'd relived most of his time with Elly, in all its Technicolor glory, and he'd woken with an unfamiliar ache under his ribs that just wouldn't shift. But right now she wasn't looking at him like he'd been featuring in any of her dreams, although perhaps he'd made an appearance in her nightmares.

'You should immunise your parents too even though they're probably not mixing with kids, unless your brother or your sister's had a child?'

The green in her eyes shimmered with barely concealed hurt; the main reason they'd separated. *You have to tell her about the children.*

But sick patients came first. The appropriate time for that story had to be finessed to avoid inflicting any more pain because he could still hear her departing words when she'd left. *I want children now, Gabe, and it's breaking my heart to love you.*

He used every strand of concentration he had to return his focus to the present because the past was full of traps. 'No, Vanessa's still in Sydney, slaying corporate dragons, and Aaron's still Aaron.' He thought of his younger brother, whose easygoing lifestyle no longer mirrored his own, and immediately switched the conversation back to the job at hand, which, although dire, was in many ways safer. 'Do you want a consult on the babies or shall I start with the backlog of walk-ins?'

'I'd appreciate the consult, thanks.'

She smiled, her face lighting up with gratitude, and unexpected sadness throbbed inside him as he realised that was all it was. Yesterday he'd thought he'd seen desire flare in her eyes but perhaps that had just been wishful thinking. He'd been doing quite a bit of that in the last sixteen hours, which made no sense because he couldn't turn back time, couldn't change how they'd hurt each other or erase what had happened to him in the intervening two years. All he knew was that he was a completely different person from the man he'd been when he'd loved Elly. It stood to reason Elly had changed too.

She started walking. 'It's a bit of a rabbit warren to the children's ward so follow me.'

The Midden Cove hospital sat high on the hill, its position garnering five-star views out across the Pacific Ocean. Like many Australian country hospitals, it had been built with money raised after the First World War specifically to care for returned servicemen. The position and spacious grounds would have been part of the plan because back in 1919 the healing qualities of sea-air had been as close to antibiotics as medicine got. Given the rising number of antibiotic-resistant bacteria, it was frightening to think that some things had come full circle.

As Gabe crossed the large built-in veranda, a shiver ran across his skin, which was crazy as it was a warm day.

Elly shot him an understanding look. 'Often at three a.m. I think I can hear the ghosts of patients past lying in their old iron beds out here.'

He tried to shrug off the feeling. 'You always did have an overactive imagination.'

She raised a questioning brow. 'Oh, right, and you don't? I saw you rub your arm.'

She'd always been incredibly observant and never missed much. *Which is why you have to tell her about the kids sooner than later.* He pulled open the door clearly labelled 'Children's Ward' and ushered her inside. 'Ironically, today we've gone back in time, dealing with an age-old illness.'

'At least we've got antibiotics.'

'True, but we both know how serious an illness this is for children under six months so we're almost as impotent as medicos were before 1945.'

They walked into the isolation ward to see a pale and haggard woman sitting next to a cot. Elly put her hand on the mother's shoulder. 'Rachel, this is Gabe Lewis. He's a...doctor too.'

Gabe heard the hesitation in her voice and

wondered what she'd dropped from the sentence. Colleague, friend, lover? Once he'd considered himself to be all of those things. Ignoring the kernel of disappointment that buried itself deep inside him, he smiled at Rachel, totally understanding her fear for her child, and then reached out to stroke Millie's head.

Recognition lit Rachel's face. 'Oh, you're Cathleen's son.'

He nodded as a rush of acid burned his stomach. *Damn small towns, where everyone knows everybody.* He tried to pre-empt the conversation and direct it away from him.

But Rachel got in first. 'I bet you're busy with—'

An incessant beeping split the air and Elly watched Gabe's expression, which had already changed from open to tense, immediately become all doctor. He firmly stimulated Millie to take a breath by blowing on her face and rubbing her chest with his hand.

'Why does that machine keep beeping?' Rachel's pinched and pale face stared up at her.

The question somehow managed to penetrate

Elly's brain, which was still spinning from the fact Gabe had greeted the baby by caressing Millie's head. The Gabe she'd known had always been slightly aloof and uncomfortable around children, but right up until the machine had announced its urgent message, he'd looked anything but uncomfortable with Millie. If anything, he'd looked uneasy with Rachel.

She hauled her concentration back to the scared mother. 'Millie's having trouble breathing and sometimes she stops for a short time, and that's called apnoea. The mattress she's lying on tells us when that happens.'

Rachel laced her fingers tightly. 'But she starts again, right? She'll always start again, won't she?'

Elly wished she could promise her that. Out of the corner of her eye she watched Gabe examining the baby, his forehead furrowed by a line as deep as a trench. 'Millie's receiving oxygen and has started on antibiotics, but she's not responding as fast as we'd hoped.'

Gabe swung his stethoscope round his neck and with eyes filled with concern he bobbed down so he was at the same height as Rachel. 'Believe me, I get how terrifying this must be for you, and Elly's done everything by the book, but Midden Cove's not equipped to handle a baby this sick. Millie's not improving, she's getting worse.'

Rachel grabbed Gabe's arms. 'What do you mean?'

'Millie's going to need assistance to breathe. The sooner we evacuate her to Hobart or Melbourne the better.'

His melodic voice that had always sounded so deep and in control when he spoke to patients suddenly had an unanticipated tone of understanding threading through it. It was as if he really *did* know how she was feeling. It all seemed surreal. First he'd touched the baby and now he had empathy she'd never seen in him before.

'What do you think, Elly?' Rachel's trembling voice immediately grounded her. 'Josh is on his way back from Launceston. Can we wait?'

She shook her head. 'I'm sorry, Rachel, but Gabe's right. Millie needs treatment by a specialist paediatrician.' She pulled her phone out of her coat pocket. 'I'm ringing the retrieval team now.'

As she spoke to the triage doctor at Royal Children's Hospital, she heard Gabe gently and carefully explaining to Rachel how the team would intubate Millie and attach her to a portable ventilator before taking off in the helicopter.

She rang off. 'They'll be here in forty minutes and, Rachel, you're going to Melbourne with her.'

Gabe immediately handed Rachel his phone. 'Ring your husband and tell him what's happening. I can talk to him if he wants that and he can ring either Elly or me at any time.'

The terrified woman nodded mutely and with trembling fingers pressed the numbers on the touch screen.

Gabe caught Elly's elbow and gently pulled her aside, his touch sparking off a traitorous wave of heat that spun through her, calling up the memory of every embrace and every kiss they'd shared.

That's just silly. Not every kiss would have been wonderful.

'Elly.'

He spoke softly and his warm breath stroked her ear. She felt her body start to sway toward him, seeking his as dangerously as a bug flying toward light. *Be strong.* She turned, which moved her slightly away from him but gave her a full view of his face. For the first time she noticed deep creases carved in around his eyes, and half-hidden in the shimmering blue was a seriousness she'd never seen before. A light shiver whooshed across her but this time she knew it wasn't a ghost.

He ran his hand through his hair. 'I'm staying with Millie until she's airlifted.'

Surprise skittered through her. Gabe was a triage specialist—assess, prioritise, organise and move on. 'One of the nurses will special her until the team arrives and we're just next door, examining the other three babies.'

He shook his head vigorously. 'You examine the other babies, send the nurse to set up the vaccination clinic in A and E and as soon as Millie leaves I'll deal with all the suspected adult cases.'

Without waiting for a reply, he turned his

attention back to Millie, examining her and re-checking that everything in the emergency intu-bation kit was ready just in case he needed it.

She'd never seen him drop the triage code like this or seen him so connected with a child. A million questions flooded her but not one could be voiced. Yet.

Six hours later, Elly came up for her first real break. The Jennings baby had been airlifted along with Millie, and the babies from the christening, although thankfully symptomless at the moment, were under close observation.

The local chapter of the Red Cross had joined forces with the state emergency service and had put together a phone-tree and a door-knock, notifying everyone of the need to come to the vaccination clinic over the next two days. Elly marvelled at how much could happen so quickly when a community pulled together.

Her phone beeped and vibrated as two text mes-sages came in. She read the first one. 'Hoping to see you this evening. Dev.'

A stab of guilt pricked her. She'd completely

forgotten to get back to him after her one word text of 'patient' she'd sent earlier in the day. Now, after the day she'd experienced, she really only wanted to go home and sink into a bubble bath and pretend that her day off had actually been relaxing. Putting off her reply to Dev, she pressed 'show message' on her phone and the second text came through. 'Just dim. U?'

She smiled and typed 'dim' on her phone, using predictive text, and got 'fin.' Some things didn't change. Gabe's fingers flew faster than his predictive text and he never checked before hitting 'Send'. She walked down to A and E and as she rounded the corner of the central desk she saw him over by the window, talking on his mobile. She waved as he looked up.

He gave a quick, tight smile loaded with tension before turning away and ploughing his left hand through his hair. She caught the words 'I won't be too much longer but only if you think can you manage.'

Manage what? A ripple of sadness washed through her, reminding her of how much everything had changed and how separate their lives really were. Once his face would have lit up when she walked into a room and he would have pulled her into his arms, phone call or not.

Come on, get a grip, don't go backwards. He obviously wanted privacy and not wishing to be accused of eavesdropping she moved away and tossed her white coat into the linen-skip. She'd just collected her bag from the bottom of the filing cabinet when Gabe appeared at the desk, pocketing his phone. His wide and generous mouth quirked up at the edges in a weary smile and again she noticed deeper lines that hadn't been there two years ago.

'So where can we go for an uninterrupted debrief?'

She hadn't expected that, especially given the phone call. 'If you need to leave we can always—'

He held up his hand. 'As colleagues, we always debriefed our cases and the fact we're no longer a couple isn't a reason to stop.' He plunged his hands into his pockets. 'But can we get out of here to do it?'

Unwanted anticipation fluttered in her stomach

and she tried to shut it down. *This was work.*
'Sure, why not? I could do with some fresh air.
Are you up for a walk?'

He grinned, the old Gabe suddenly front and
centre. 'Sounds good to me.'

They strolled through the hospital gardens, past
the massed silver-bush plants with their cheery
white flowers and silver-grey leaves, and then
they turned toward the beach; two doctors discussing their cases, rethinking their treatment op-
tions and learning from pooling their thoughts.

Elly automatically turned left at a spindly tree
and walked into the picnic area-cum-children's
playground nestled in the dunes above the sea
wall. It was a popular place for families as the
tidal river on this side of the bridge was quiet
compared with further downstream where an
eddying rip swirled at the tidal junction. She
loved to sit on the sea wall and watch the parade
of yachts, their brightly coloured spinnakers
bulging in the wind as they raced between the
channel markers, but most of all she loved to
listen to the children's shrieks of delight as they

played on the swings and play equipment or on the beach below.

Often children would come and chat to her, holding up their buckets and proudly showing off their soldier crabs and periwinkles. Even though she knew it was a crazy daydream, she sometimes pretended she was part of it and was at the beach with her own children. *One day.* She bit her lip. She'd been telling herself that now for over two years and she wasn't any closer.

Dev says he wants children.

Unease sat like a rock in her gut. The thought that had held tempting appeal last night seemed slightly tarnished in the full sunshine of daylight.

Gabe stopped suddenly, and did a rapid one-eighty-degree scan of the area as waves of tension rolled off him like sea-fog.

'Something wrong?'

His sunglasses hid his eyes as he patted down his pockets and then with an audible sound of relief he produced his phone. 'Sorry, for a moment I thought I'd left it at the hospital.'

She remembered seeing him slide it into his

pocket back at the desk and at the time she'd been slightly puzzled by the uncharacteristic self-conscious look he'd given her. She'd put it down to one of those uncomfortable moments ex-lovers had. But this reaction to the phone snagged her. She'd known him to lose things in the past and barely react to their loss, other than saying, 'It'll turn up eventually.' It was another jar, another change in him, and they were starting to form a list—his reaction to Millie, his empathy with Rachel, the deep lines around his mouth and eyes, and now this.

'For someone on holidays, you seem a bit strung out.'

'Nah.' He grinned and winked; his blue-on-blue eyes sparkling and his gaze so direct and all-encompassing it was as if she was the absolute centre of his world.

Careful. She recognised his flirting look of old but it gave her scant immunity as she tried unsuccessfully to steel herself against the traitorous tendrils that wove through her.

The mangled strains of 'Greensleeves' drifted across on the summer breeze and Gabe abruptly turned and started striding out of the park, making his way toward the music and calling over his shoulder, 'Do you want an ice cream?'

It took her brain a moment to catch up and her legs even longer, and by the time she arrived at the van he'd already ordered her favourite: a lemon gelato.

'Enjoy.' He handed her a waffle cone bulging with two enormous scoops of the tangy confection.

'Thanks.'

'Let's sit over here.' He tilted his head away from the park and the late-afternoon sunshine picked up the straw colour of his hair, making it dazzle like golden thread. A golden god visiting the mortals.

Elly looked at the Norfolk pines and their prickly fallen scale-like leaves and said, 'Let's not. The sea wall's much prettier.'

Wariness crossed his face. 'There are more people there.'

'Are you worried we'll be seen? Fear not, one ice cream with me won't ruin your free-and-easy bachelor reputation.' She licked her ice cream and started strolling to cover her jab of disappointment.

He fell into step with her. 'That's not what I meant. I just thought it would be good to have somewhere quiet to talk rather than a park full of tearaway toddlers.'

Now, that was more like the Gabe she remembered. 'Rest easy, mate. It's past six and any self-respecting toddler is at home, having dinner and a bath.' And she was right. The park was virtually empty, and a small group of teenagers left the moment Elly and Gabe walked in.

But for someone who had wanted to talk, Gabe was strangely silent as they dangled their legs over the sea wall and ate their ice cream. When they'd had work to discuss they'd had conversation but they'd well and truly debriefed and now there was just awkwardness, an almost tangible bubble of distance bulging between them. This must be the ex factor. This was the sum of all their time apart and different dreams. This afternoon she'd realised that Gabe had changed and she guessed she must have too.

We've both moved on.

Melancholy circled her heart but at least now she knew for sure there was nothing left between them. The moment she finished her ice cream she was going home. She'd have that bath. Her niggling conscience said, *You should ring Dev.*

A cold, wet sensation crossed her hand and with a start she realised her now-melting gelato was dripping. 'Oh, *ick*, I'm getting all sticky.' She held it up high and gave it a giant lick around the perimeter of the cone. Liquid ran down her jaw.

Gabe laughed. 'Some things don't change. You were always hopeless with ice cream.' He leaned forward, his hand gently cupping her jaw while his thumb slowly swept across her chin.

She stilled at the touch that should have been practical and prosaic yet was anything but. Tingles shot through her, making her tremble from head to toe. *Stop it and get with the programme. You heard, we've moved on! S*he tried valiantly to claim back control and she swallowed. Hard.

Intense, light blue eyes instantly darkened to navy, holding her gaze transfixed as if it was bonded to her. His head moved slowly toward hers.

Pull back now! Maintain distance! But she stayed perfectly still. She no longer cared what was sensible or logical; she just wanted him to kiss her *one* more time to prove that it really was all over between them. Call it an experiment. She was a doctor, a scientist and she needed to know if she'd been living on memories overblown by time and longing. Memories that had interfered with every attempt at a new relationship. Now she had a chance for reality to finally reveal those memories as fraudulent and then she and her traitorous body could truly move forward.

His five-o'clock shadow brushed her cheek as his scent of good health and fresh pine swirled around her. She tilted her head so his lips brushed hers. Like a jolt of electricity buzzing through her body, tingles and shimmers raced through her, quickly chased by heat. Wondrous, glorious heat that set her alight and demanded more. Much more.

His tongue traced the outline of her lips and with a moan she opened her mouth as her hand released the ice cream to the sand below. He tasted of spearmint and chocolate and home. His mouth covered hers without a hint of hesitation, knowing exactly where to go and what to do to make her his, and, God help her, she never wanted it to stop.

The noise of car doors slamming, seagulls squawking and gentle waves lapping faded away as every part of her was absorbed by the kiss. She wanted to invade his mouth and reclaim it as hers, but his stroking lips derailed her so instead she gloried in his urgent pressure of desire, his softness of seduction and the intensity of his lust.

Ribbons of pure pleasure unfurled, streaming through her and stripping her bones of strength. She leaned into him for support and felt him tremble. As if reading her mind, one hand cupped the back of her head as the other pushed her shoulder and they tumbled gently back onto the grassy knoll.

His lips slid off hers for a moment and as he stared down at her a million undefined emotions flashed in his eyes. 'God, I've missed you.'

Her heart quivered as his husky voice filled her with desperate yearning and hope. 'I've missed you, too.' Her hands pulled him closer, needing to touch him, needing to feel the tautness of his muscles against her skin and his leg entwining with hers as he lay half against her.

His hand slid under her blouse, seeking her breast, which ached for his touch. His fingers touched the hard nipple and she gasped as a rainbow of colours showered her mind. Now her tongue invaded his mouth, taking what she knew belonged to her, and she revelled in her power as he shuddered against her.

Sand trickled into her waistband, grass prickled her heels but she hardly noticed as her fingers traced the length of his spine, the touch and feel so familiar to her that she knew the outline of every bone and crevice and exactly where to press to make him tremble.

As if on cue, he groaned against her and his mouth trailed down her neck; nipping, branding, kissing and whispering words that ignited the last remnants of longing into raging need. She never wanted it to end.

'Daddy!'

Gabe stiffened and instantly broke the kiss.

She vaguely heard the sweet call of a child's voice, immediately followed by deeper adult tones, and she reached out to touch his cheek. 'I guess you're right. This is getting way out of hand for a public park so let's go back to my place.'

He made a guttural sound and rolled away from her.

Warm air rushed in, making her feel cold after the raging heat of their bodies, and her desire-hazed vision instantly cleared. Shock scarred his handsome face, giving it a haggardness she'd never seen before, and her blood turned to ice. 'What's wrong, what's happened?'

'Daddy!'

A toddler threw himself at Gabe, who hastily rose to his feet, swinging the child easily up into his arms. 'Hey, honey-pie.'

Daddy? Honey-pie?

Elly's chest constricted so tightly she couldn't get air in or out, and her stomach contents rose in a bile-filled wave, threatening to expel themselves.

I don't want children, El, it's just not me.

Blood roared in her ears and her head spun. Somehow she managed to stand up, forcing her legs to hold her rigidly upright. She stared at the blonde little girl with blue-on-blue eyes, whose head rested so easily and trustingly against Gabe's chest. 'You...you have a child?'

'Elly.' Her name came out on a strangled plea. 'Please, I can—'

'Daddy! Daddy!'

Elly swung around to see two identical dark-haired little boys making a bee-line for Gabe, followed by Gabe's parents. A cry of anguish stalled in her throat and her right hand gripped her chest as piercing pain ripped through her, sparing no part of her. She turned back to look at the child in Gabe's arms as the twins threw themselves at his knees.

She swayed as the world started to spin. *Oh, God, how could this be happening?*

Gabe had three children, all under two. Triplets.

CHAPTER FOUR

'ELLY, don't look like that.'

Pure white had more colour in it than her face. Convinced she was going to faint, Gabe shot out his spare hand, wrapping it firmly around her waist.

She shook his hand free, her bright green eyes filled with loathing and betrayal as she mouthed the words, 'You bastard.'

He wanted to yell, *It's your fault—you left me and set this in all in motion.* But that wouldn't solve a thing. Enough guilt swirled inside him to acknowledge that despite everything that had happened between them, Elly didn't deserve to have found out about the triplets this way. He'd been about to tell her when she'd spilled her gelato, but the moment his thumb had touched her chin, and her eyes had glowed with the same longing that blazed inside him, all coherent thought had vanished.

Her eyes had sparkled with their shared past, and he'd glimpsed happier times when his life had been simple and straightforward. Despite knowing too much had gone down between them for them ever to return to being a couple, for one brief and crazy moment he'd desperately wanted it all back so much it hurt. And he'd wanted her. All of her.

Seriously bad timing for the libido to come back, mate. He'd foolishly ignored common sense and taken what she'd offered, and in the process had inflicted serious damage.

'Let me explain.'

She shook her head, her jaw rigid and her mouth silent.

'Gabe, give Lucy to me. Boys, run to Pa-pa.' His mother reached out her arms, her expression a mixture of confusion and concern. 'Hello, Elly.'

'Cathleen, James.' Elly's words were barely audible as she tilted her head in a jerky greeting.

'I'm sorry, but I need to leave.' She started to walk rapidly toward the road.

Panic thundered through Gabe. He couldn't let her leave, not like this, and he threw an imploring look at his parents.

They nodded their understanding but many un-asked questions lingered in their eyes. Gathering the children, they started walking toward the beach steps. 'Let's dig for crabs and Daddy will come soon and count them all.'

With the kids safe and sorted, he ran, his chest aching, his brain spinning, trying to work out the best way to deal with this mess. He reached her just as she turned out of the park. 'Elly, I'm sorry.'

She didn't respond, just kept speed-walking with her gaze fixed straight ahead and anguish rolling off her like crashing surf pounding against sand.

He ran his hand through his hair, regret and pain burning inside him. 'I never planned for you to find out this way. In fact, I was trying to tell you just before.'

She stopped so suddenly she almost toppled

forward and her gaze swung toward him, her eyes firing daggers. 'Kissing me isn't telling me you're a father. Or was that part of the plan, Gabe? Kiss me senseless, get me into bed and then in the post-coital haze you just drop in the line— *Oh, by the way, I have triplets.*'

'No, of course not.' Indignation flared out of guilt. 'I admit the kiss was a mistake.'

Oh, yeah, saying that's really going to help. Just shut up!

But the warning came too late and her body twitched as if shocked. 'Well, at least we're on the same page, then. Everything about that kiss was a mistake. Everything about *us* was and is a mistake.' A sigh shuddered out of her. 'I don't want to talk to you, Gabe. Just go back to *your* family.'

The vitriol in her voice shocked him and he reached for her hand, desperate to connect with her in some way, desperate to state his case. 'I know you're angry, Elly, hell you have every right to be, but you also deserve to know the whole story.'

She peeled his hand away from hers, her touch

ice-cold. 'I'm not going to appease your guilt by allowing you to tell me anything.'

Her words vibrated deep inside him, striking both a perfect chord and a discordant clash. Nothing was ever simple and, damn it, she'd walked out of *his* life, but for some crazy reason he felt he owed her the truth. 'What if wanting to tell you isn't about me at all but about you?'

She crossed her arms tightly over her chest, as if she was physically holding herself together. 'We broke up, Gabe, and what you did with your life after that has nothing to do with me. Absolutely nothing.' She started walking up the hill as a car came round the bend.

You left me! But he pushed that pain away because one of them had to approach this in a non-emotive manner. He reached for her again, his hand resting gently on her shoulder. 'Nothing to do with you? I don't think you believe that.'

Her steps faltered and she hesitated as the crunching sounds of gravel under tyres sounded loud and close. A car pulled off the road, coming to a halt next to them. The door opened and the bloke he'd met briefly at the yacht-club dinner, Dev someone, got out, his gaze stretching tautly between the two of them. 'Eleanor, are you OK?'

'She's fine.' He hated the way this guy was looking at Elly. 'If you'll excuse us, we're in the middle of having a private conversation.' The words exploded in a primal growl from deep inside him, like a wolf protecting his mate.

Elly quickly stepped forward out from under his touch and reached for the passenger doorhandle. 'Take me home.'

Dev nodded. 'Get in.'

'Elly, wait.' He hated the anger-tinged pleading in his voice.

Dev gave Gabe a victorious sneer that said, *This is my woman*, and slid back into the car. He took off in a spin of gravel.

Fury, despair and sadness churned through him, along with an unwanted and completely irrational streak of emerald-green jealousy. How had trying to do the right and honourable thing come to this?

* * *

Elly couldn't get warm. Despite the balmy summer evening and layers of clothing, she couldn't stop shivering. The doctor in her knew she was in shock and she tried to sip hot, sweet tea, but her hands trembled so much she risked scalding herself. The last hour had been the slowest of her life. Somehow she'd managed to convince Dev she was exhausted and needed sleep. She'd watched him unhappily stifle his many questions and leave but she knew he expected an explanation sooner rather than later.

She could just imagine the conversation. *Who's Gabe?*

Oh, just an ex-lover who with one kiss had me on my back and almost naked in a public park. You know, the sort of sexual sizzle you and I just don't have.

She dropped her head in her hands. What a mess. She should never have complicated things by asking Dev to drive her home but she'd been desperate to get away from Gabe. She hadn't been able to process anything he'd been saying because all she'd been able to think about had been three little children.

I don't want children, El, it's just not me.

Her chest cramped with betrayal as piercing pain shot through her and the shaking restarted. She struggled for a way through this, a way to claw back some semblance of control.

Facts. *You're a scientist, just deal with known facts.*

Gabe was a father.

His duplicity burned through her like acid, eating away at her, and with every hot spot more questions burned her. The Gabe she'd loved had always been honest and she'd trusted him implicitly. Well, she had until an hour ago when everything had changed.

Honest? He didn't tell you about the children.

He said he'd been trying.

She recalled the awkward silence just before he'd kissed her and she realised he'd spoken the truth. Like a jigsaw coming together, she suddenly recognised that the changes in him that had snagged her had actually been hints—his behaviour toward Millie, his reaction to the park, him wanting to sit under the pines to talk. He'd wanted to tell her and he'd been working up to doing it.

As her shock moved from mind-numbing fury to clinging to facts in an attempt to make sense of the situation, she grudgingly recognised how hard it would be for him to tell her. *Come on, get real. He bailed on the hard truth and kissed you instead.*

A jet of anger spiked up again, its white heat consuming her. She couldn't forgive him for that. Sure, Gabe enjoyed a party and a good time but not once in their year together had she ever entertained the idea he had been cheating on her. When he'd kissed her today she'd interpreted that as him being free to kiss her. Obviously he was far from free.

You more than kissed him back and technically you're not one hundred per cent free.

Like a pin to a balloon, her self-righteous indignation deflated. Last night she'd told Dev she wanted to try a serious relationship with him and less than twenty-four hours later she was not only kissing another man, she'd invited him into her bed, her body desperate to have him all. God, she was just as bad as Gabe.

The word 'mess' didn't seem strong enough to accurately describe this shambles. She gulped down the now-cooler tea, feeling the sugar sweeping through her, slightly steadying her see-sawing emotions.

Gabe is a father.

She didn't realise four words could hurt so much.

'Gabe is a father.' She spoke the words out loud, needing to hear them to help them sink in, to help her face a new reality. *And?*

She knew the answer to that question. As Gabe was a father, that fact alone meant there was a woman who was a mother. A woman he was connected to for ever. Did she want to know? *No!*

Yes!

No, it's only going to hurt. She didn't think she could take any more pain so could she just ignore the whole situation?

Really? You're going to ignore it?

Of course she could. She'd lived without Gabe

in her life for two years and his arrival here didn't change anything. Not. One. Thing.

With that decision made, she ran a bath and tipped in lavender and chamomile by the bucket-load. As she lay under the warm, fragrant water, breathing in the calming aromas and concentrating on long, slow breaths in and out, she willed herself to let go of the last hour's events. Nothing about Gabe's life had any impact on her. Nothing at all.

You are so deluding yourself.

She slipped lower in the water, so every part of her except her head was submerged; forcing her mind to float above everything, telling herself that nothing about Gabe's life choices could touch her or hurt her.

He didn't love you enough to want to have children with you.

She gasped as another wave of pain hit her. Was this the truth? Had he lied to her when she'd asked him to commit to her and a family? Tears burned her eyes, the pain even more fierce than when she'd found out about the children.

She pulled herself to her feet and grabbed

a towel. There was no possible way could she ignore this. She had to know. Now. With jerky movements, she somehow managed to dry some of the moisture off her body before tugging on the nearest clothes, which happened to be loose, bright, Asian 'happy' pants. The irony wasn't lost on her.

Stumbling into her cork-lined slides, she opened her front door and stepped into the night. She didn't care what time it was or that she'd stormed away from Gabe, telling him she never wanted to hear the story. She still didn't want 'the story'. All she wanted was the facts. The only way for her to process all of this, to put it behind her so she could move forward, was with the facts.

Cold, emotionless facts.

He owed her that.

Gabe had counted crabs, washed three tired and sandy children and had a shocking time getting them to go to sleep. He knew why they'd been so hard to settle—they were reacting to his complete distraction. He tried to give them his full attention but Elly's ashen face and her expression of abject betrayal kept running through his head, always closely followed by the fact she'd got into that car.

Did you think she hadn't got on with her life? She invited me to her place!

God, she'd kissed like a wicked angel, reminding him that her mouth had always been the most seductive one he'd ever kissed.

Kissing her was a mistake. Not only because she hates you, but you so don't need or want a woman in your life adding to the chaos.

For the hundredth time he ploughed his hand through a well-worn path in his hair. Kissing her had been a moment of weakness he couldn't afford. Even though he and Elly didn't have a future, he couldn't leave things like this between them. He knew she wouldn't return calls even though he'd left two messages, and flowers were not going to work. He had to go and see her and risk the door being slammed in his face.

He stuck his head into the lounge room where his parents were watching TV. 'The kids are finally asleep.'

His mother put her cross-stitch down on her

lap and looked straight at him. 'How well do you know Elly Ruddock?'

'Well enough.' His hand tightened on the architrave. He'd never shared his personal life with his parents because they'd always been half-way round the world, and mentioning a girlfriend who would probably have a different name the next time they enquired meant it had been easier not to say anything. But things had changed and because of the triplets, his parents were very involved in his life and that took some getting used to. Right now he wasn't prepared to go into the full story. Not until he'd sorted things out with Elly.

His mother frowned. 'And she didn't know about the triplets?'

He shook his head. 'But she does now. Look, I'm just ducking out for a walk. Thought I'd call into the pub and put the word out about the whooping-cough vaccination.'

His father gave him a sage look. 'Tread carefully.'

He rolled his eyes. 'Midden Cove is hardly King's St, Melbourne, Dad.'

'It has its own dangers, Gabe. William Congreve knew what he was talking about.'

Gabe caught the obscure reference to 'Hell hath no fury like a woman scorned' and thought that wrath was probably a lot less than what Elly was feeling.

'I've got a key, don't wait up.' He let himself out into the night, and struck out toward Elly's cottage.

Midden Cove didn't run to much by way of streetlighting once off the main road, so he navigated by the bright moonlight. The gentle thump of a calm ocean washing over sand wafted through the air, the sound almost meditative. In other circumstances a night walk might be something he could do just to get some time to himself. He loved the kids more than life itself but between them and work there was nothing left just for him.

The noise of footsteps on gravel made him look up and he thought he could make out a woman's figure walking toward him, but then he was blinded by a very bright and white LED torch.

His arms shot up to shield his eyes. 'Would you mind lowering the beam?'

'Gabe?' The beam wobbled.

'Yes, it's me, Elly.'

'I was coming to see you.'

They spoke at the same moment, their words tumbling over each other; a deep melody singing with clear soprano tones.

Thank you. He was going to get his opportunity to explain because she wanted to listen. 'I'd suggest we go to my parents' place to talk but—'

'Here is just fine.' She turned off the torch.

'Um, we're in the middle of the road, El.'

'It's Midden Cove.' Her voice sounded ragged, as if she was using every ounce of strength to stay composed.

O-K... 'Thanks for coming. We need to have this talk and—'

'I think I hate you, Gabe.' She started shaking uncontrollably, her hair falling forward across her face. 'You were so adamant you didn't want kids and now...I truly and honestly hate you.'

Her anguish rammed into him. Without thinking, he closed the gap between them, wrapping his arms around her and pulling her against him. He hated himself for having caused all this pain, pain for Elly, pain for Jenna and heartache for himself. He buried his face in her hair and breathed in deeply.

She stilled under his touch for a second, her body against his, her curves hugging his own as if they'd been designed as two parts that fitted together in a perfect match. Then every muscle turned rigid, her hands balled into fists against his chest and she pushed back, making both of them stumble.

She raised traumatised eyes to his. 'What are their names?'

Oh, God, this was going to be awful. 'Elly, let's go somewhere private to do this.'

'No. We're doing this my way. I'm asking the questions and you're answering them.' Her voice came through clenched teeth. 'What. Are. Their. Names?'

Memories of past arguments came back to him, with both of them intransigent and deaf to the other. This time it had to be different so despite feeling like he was in the dock and being cross-examined, he forced himself to go along with her for now, hoping she'd relax and then they could relocate to somewhere more suitable. 'Lucy, Ben and Rory.'

'Nice names.'

'Thanks. I think so.' The air around them swirled with strained politeness that barely rose above the simmering base emotion of raw and ragged pain.

She started to pace. 'So, they're twins and a spare?'

He nodded at the accurate description of the triplets as he caught her muttered 'What are the odds?'

The answer was engraved on his heart and soul, having looked it up ten thousand times at least in the days after he'd first stared at the grainy ultrasound image. 'A one in eight thousand chance, actually.'

She bit her lip and kept moving. 'Exactly how old are they?'

The urge to protect her warred with the truth, which was insane because she'd seen the triplets and any doctor could fairly accurately diagnose a child under five's approximate age. 'Fifteen months.'

She stopped walking and a short sound shot from her lips, jagging through him.

'Elly.' He reached for her but she swung away.

'Don't touch me.' Her arms crossed her chest, making a physical barrier. 'I've only come here for the facts. I trusted you, Gabe. I believed you when you told me you didn't want children but that was wrong, wasn't it? You just didn't want to have children with *me* because you had plans with the other woman you were sleeping with.'

Her words stung like a sharp slap, sparking a flare of resentment that she could believe he'd do something so low. 'I *never* cheated on you, Elly.'

Her tight face said she didn't believe him. 'Do the maths, Gabe.'

'Do the medicine, El.' His jaw ached as he ground out the words. 'They were born six weeks early, as most triplets are.'

She stiffened and resumed pacing. 'Who's their mother?'

He sighed and realised he always did when he talked about the mother of his children. 'Jenna. Jenna Pardy. I doubt you've ever met her.'

'But you did, what, a month after we broke up?' For the first time her voice had a hysterical edge.

He shrugged as his enforced calm started to fracture. 'You and I, we'd broken up. We weren't on a break, we were *over*. In fact, they were *your* words when you left the apartment, even though I'd asked you to reconsider.'

He'd thought he had an handle on his hurt that she hadn't loved him enough to stay but simmering anger burst up from deep inside him; a burning rage at her for leaving him and setting all of this mess in motion. 'Let the jury note that I was very single when I met Jenna.'

She swung back to him, her face translucent in the moonlight. 'So what happened to your condom obsession or was it Jenna who changed your mind?'

'I *thought* we were using contraception.' Resentment against Jenna's deception spun into his anger as he revisited a question he'd asked himself a million times. He sucked in a deep breath, battling a vortex of emotions, and tried again to be the rational one. 'Look, Elly, I know you're hurting and I know this is hard for you, but I need to tell you the whole story my way. In a way that makes sense rather than you peppering me with random questions.'

Fear streaked across her face. 'No! I don't want to hear everything, I can't hear everything. I can only deal with the facts.'

He threw his hands out wide, his patience so thin it hung by a thread. 'This is crazy and I'm not going to discuss it with you under these conditions.'

'Did you marry her?' She asked the question so quietly he almost missed it.

Gabe, you'll never guess. The memory of a wildly ecstatic Jenna shoving a positive pregnancy test into his hand flooded back, along with his appalled shock. 'She was pregnant with my children.'

'I'll take that as a yes, then.' With trembling fingers Elly tucked her hair behind her ears.

'That's all I need to know. Goodbye, Gabe.' She started to walk away.

The last vestiges of his controlled restraint fell to his feet. Bitterness surged in at her intractable manner, combining with old but vivid memories of the time she'd walked out on him two years ago. He was done with being cast as the bad guy, done with trying to protect her feelings. 'Damn it all to hell, Elly, that is nowhere near close to what you need to know.'

CHAPTER FIVE

ELLY felt Gabe's acrimony barrel into her but she kept walking, her own anger and grief driving her on as she called back over her shoulder, 'It's all *I* want to know.'

'And that's your style, isn't it, Elly? You want everything your own way and you walk when it doesn't happen.'

His words hit like shrapnel, spraying through her in a barrage of pain. *Ignore him, he's wrong.* 'That's a ridiculous accusation.'

'Really?'

'Yes, really. I don't need to have everything my own way.'

His grim laugh was pure distain. 'Who left our apartment?'

She refused to stop and look at him but she could picture him with his arms crossed and his square jaw vibrating with fury. 'It was *your* apartment, Gabe, and I left because I wanted a family and you didn't.'

His feet crunched the gravel and he caught up with her but he didn't try and touch her. 'And that's how you remember it?'

She tried not to breathe deeply as his freshly showered scent spun around her. 'Of course it's how I remember it because it's exactly what happened. You said, "I don't want children, El."'

He grunted in disbelief. 'No, that isn't what I said at all.'

A questioning chill ran through her veins but she rubbed her arms and kept on walking. 'Oh, right, so now you're reinventing history and telling me you actually wanted children.'

'I said I didn't want children *then*.' The words came out in a warning growl.

Her brain ached and seeds of doubt tried to sprout but she refused to let them. 'That's not what I heard, and if you did actually say that then what about the whole "it's just not me"?'

His long stride had no problem keeping up with her. 'Damn it, Elly, you hit me with the whole baby thing completely out of the blue, and I was honest enough to tell you the truth that existed for me at that point. You took it and twisted it around because it wasn't what you wanted to hear.'

No, he's wrong and I'm right. I have to be right. She shook her head so hard her brain hurt. 'There's no point even discussing this with you because it's in the past and we've both moved on with our lives.' She almost broke into a jog.

'That's right, run. Go right ahead and maintain your moral high ground, Elly. It's so much easier to hide behind that than face the truth that you might be wrong. Only this time why not add in your preconceived ideas about me and the triplets to fire your disdain.' The fury in his voice burned the air around them. 'And while you're walking, you might just want to consider this—it isn't all about you and you're not the only person hurting here.'

His ragged voice acted like glue on her feet and she stopped walking, even though she didn't want to. Turning slowly, she saw his face in the moonlight; haggard with deep lines and crevices that had appeared during the time they'd been separated. Her heart bled.

Keep going. He broke your heart, and to-night he's stomped on it. But her feet refused to move.

He gripped his forehead, his thumb and fore-finger pressing into his temples. 'I know you feel ill used, Elly, and hard done by, but do you seriously think you had the most to lose when we separated?'

Yes! Her pain and anguish swirled inside her. 'I lost… I wanted… You had…' Her throat closed against words that struggled to be spoken as the truth spluttered like a newly lit candle, and slowly took hold until it glowed bright and tall with un-assailable clarity.

Sharp, red-hot pain tore through her, stealing the breath from her lungs. She really *did* think she'd lost the most. But she could see clearly on his face that he'd suffered too. She closed her eyes for a moment, trying to find her equilibrium, but it evaded her and everything felt unsteady. Had his life been turned on its head as much as hers by their separation?

He met Jenna.

She tried to hold on to the bitter emotions that

he'd met someone so quickly but they collided with his recently spoken words. *We were over. In fact, they were your words.*

What about your own dating spree? A jagged pain made her want to curl up. For all this time she'd only been able to see her own hurt. How had she not realised she'd hurt him?

Because you didn't want to think about it.

She'd been so angry with him and then so bereft that her life had become empty of intimacy and her dream of a family was still only a dream that she'd never really thought about him being devastated by their parting. Dear God, what a selfish princess she'd been. The uncomfortable truth pounded her, demanding she at least acknowledge his feelings.

She raised her eyes, taking in his haggard face. 'You're right. All this time I've been thinking I was the one who lost the most.'

He flinched. 'So the fact that I declared my *then* love for you and asked you to stay and give me some time didn't count because really you didn't believe me?'

She bit her lip as his pain circled her like razor

wire. She spoke softly, finding it hard to get the words out. 'I knew you loved me.'

'But not that I'd change my mind?'

I need a yes or no answer, Gabe. The suppressed memory of the minutiae of that night two years ago surfaced. She'd backed the most stubborn man she'd ever met into a corner and he'd come out swinging. *'I don't want children now. El, it's just not me right now but who knows down the track? All I can give you now is a maybe.'*

She hadn't been able to invest in 'down the track' or 'maybe'. A wave of sorrow washed over her and she realised she'd thrown the love he'd once had for her back in his face. 'You're right. I believed you wouldn't change your mind and that if I waited I'd lose precious time to meet someone who wanted a family as much as I did.' A sound that mangled a laugh and a cry came from her throat. 'Pretty ironic really, given the circumstances.'

'Yeah, I suppose it is.' He sounded tired and immensely sad, as if he had no energy left to argue with her. 'Look, about that kiss...'

My then love. A wave of embarrassing heat

flushed through her and she held up her hand like a stop sign. She didn't want him to say anything more about the kiss or the fact she'd so quickly suggested they continue in her bed. 'It's OK, I get it. Sometimes memories swamp us but it was a bad idea.'

'Yeah.'

'Let's not talk about it again.'

'Good idea.'

A heavy silence wrapped around them both and a different sort of pain—one of lost opportunities and deep regret—filled her with an amplified sense of loss. Who knew what might have happened if she'd been more patient and prepared to wait? But there was no point going there because Gabe now had a wife and a family.

You can make amends, though.

She swallowed hard and forced out the words she needed to say. 'You're right, I do need to listen and let you tell you me all about your life with Jenna and the children.'

His strong, broad shoulders seemed to sag for a moment as if weighed down by melancholy, and she had to hold herself back from hugging him.

He met her gaze, his eyes disconcertingly empty. 'Is there somewhere quiet we can go other than your place?'

She nodded, realising the two of them alone was a bad idea. She opened her mouth to reply but his mobile rang; the sound loud and jarring.

He answered it, his free hand tugging at his hair as he listened intently before saying, 'I'll be home in five.' He rang off. 'Sorry, I have to go. Lucy's running a temp.'

'Do you want me to see her?' The offer came out impulsively, as if she didn't know he was a doctor.

He shook his head. 'She's teething and although none of the textbooks say kids get a fever, I can tell you now—they can. That and filthy nappies.' His attempt at a smile didn't quite reach his eyes and a sigh shuddered through him. 'Are you right to get home?'

She nodded. 'Sure, it's not far.' *Be a grown-up with him.* 'Perhaps I could formally meet every-one to make things less strained?'

His eyes suddenly stared down into hers for

a moment and she saw real heartache before shutters came down fast.

'My life's complicated, Elly.'

She bit her lip as she deciphered the distancing code embedded in the sentence. *And you're no longer part of it.*

'What on earth's happened to you?' Elly's friend Sarah passed her a cup of tea in the small church-hall kitchen. 'You look like you've seen a ghost— or has Dev finally bored you so much that you've turned into a zombie?'

Elly had just arrived at the playgroup, having come to give an information session about the whooping-cough epidemic. But Sarah had taken one look at her and hustled her off into the kitchen.

'Seriously, Elly, you look terrible. Are you sure you shouldn't be home in bed?'

She thought of the emotional roller-coaster she'd ridden in the last thirty-six hours and wasn't sure where to begin or if she really wanted to. 'You're kind of right. I have seen a ghost, a ghost of boyfriends past in the guise of Gabe Lewis.'

Sarah's eyes widened with interest. 'Dr Gabe? James and Cathleen's totally hunky son is an ex?'

She sucked down the wave of pain. 'Not just any ex. *The* ex.'

'The guy who didn't want kids?' Sarah sat down hard on a chair, shock clear on her face. 'But he's got—'

Elly flinched and cut her off. 'Triplets. Yes, I know. A ready-made family.'

'Oh, hell, Elly, I'm sorry.' She suddenly glanced nervously out through the window into the play area. 'Um, Elly, the triplets came to playgroup today. Are you sure you're up to facing all this?'

His children are here. She bit her lip and then remembered with relief that Gabe wouldn't be there. He'd texted her that morning to say he was still keeping his promise to do the vaccination clinic from ten until noon.

Jenna will be here.

My life is complicated.

Curiosity intertwined with heartache as she realised this talk might be the one opportunity she got to see the mother of Gabe's children. Not that she wanted to talk to her but she wanted to see her because it would make the whole situation real and surely that had to help her deal with the bombshell that had exploded in her face yesterday.

She rolled her shoulders back. 'The town needs me to do this talk so you organise the parents inside, and I'll do my job. It'll be fine.'

Sarah didn't look quite convinced.

An hour later Elly was hoarse from fielding questions but she believed she'd lowered the anxiety levels and reduced the general panic. But she hadn't seen anyone she didn't know, hadn't seen Jenna. Sarah publicly thanked her and invited people to join in the communal morning tea, but Elly forced herself to walk outside to the play area, wanting to see if Jenna was there. After all, her husband was a doctor so she'd already know about whooping cough and had probably skipped the talk.

She scanned the garden. Two teenage girls were playing games with the littlies, having minded them so their parents, mostly mothers, could attend her session, and there were two other adults as well. With a start, she recognised them to be Gabe's parents. James was sitting in the sandpit with a little boy on each side and Cathleen was watching Lucy splashing with the water-play set. She swung her head around to take in the entire area but there were no other adults present. Jenna wasn't there.

Cathleen gave her a tentative smile and beckoned Elly over. 'I'm sorry we didn't come to your talk but with our mob we thought we should stay and help the girls, and Gabe had filled us in on the situation.'

Situation? A strand of panic spun through her. Which situation? Whooping cough or the fact she and Gabe had once been a couple?

If Cathleen noticed that Elly was struck mute she didn't show it and she continued with, 'Those poor little babies.'

It's the whooping-cough situation. Elly quickly recovered, latching onto the topic like a lifeline. 'I spoke with the paediatrician this morning and both are still critical but neither have deteriorated any further, which gives us hope.'

'That's a bit of good news, then.' Gabe's mother glanced over at Lucy. 'Grandchildren are so precious.'

Elly's heart cramped. 'All children are precious.'

'Very true.' Cathleen's serious expression suddenly lightened. 'Elly, James and I have organised all the bags and gloves for the next Coast-Care clean-up and the T-shirts arrived yesterday. They look fantastic and James's business associate in Melbourne donated them so that's even better.'

Glad to be talking about something completely neutral, Elly gave Cathleen a wide thank-you smile. 'That's great news. We'll all look sensational as we haul rubbish. So, will you bring all the gear down to the beach at seven on Saturday morning?'

Cathleen frowned. 'Actually, with the triplets being here, life's a bit unpredictable at the moment.' As if right on cue, Cathleen's attention was suddenly pulled away by Lucy, who'd abandoned the water play and was heading for a trike. 'Could you collect them before Saturday and that way we know they're going to get to the right place at the right time?'

My life is complicated, Elly. The last thing she wanted to do was call by the Lewis house and risk meeting Gabe, who didn't want to see her and would think she'd come to meet Jenna. 'What if James—?'

But Cathleen wasn't listening as she rushed to intercept Lucy, who was heading straight for a bike much too big for her. She helped the child up onto a toddler-sized trike and called out to Elly, 'Come after six tonight—that would work best.'

For the first time in her life, Elly wished she wasn't a Coast-Care volunteer.

Gabe had three highchairs in a semicircle, and three hungry toddlers sat impatiently waiting for their dinner.

'More,' Rory demanded.

'Juice.' Lucy pointed to the orange juice container.

Ben, the quietest of the three, started to bang

his spoon on the tray top. The others immediately joined in.

'It's coming.' He sliced up sausages and distributed them over three plastic plates.

'Nana. Nana.' Lucy looked expectantly beyond the kitchen.

'Nana and Pa-pa have gone to a concert, remember. We waved bye-bye to the car and that's why Daddy cooked the barbecue.' He drizzled tomato sauce over the sausages and dumped a mixture of carrot and capsicum sticks next to them before placing a plate in front of each bibbed child.

The silence was deafening and he smiled. Some children didn't eat but his all had healthy appetites, although Ben sometimes had to be encouraged. It was for that reason he'd chosen sausages tonight because they were Ben's favourite and as he was doing the entire frantic evening routine on his own, he'd gone for simplicity. Simple pretty much matched his culinary skills. He handed each of them a non-spill sippy cup filled with some diluted juice. 'What do you say?'

'Ta.' Rory smiled.

'Juice.' Lucy nodded.

Ben grinned and said, 'Jubba jubba jubba,' which Gabe always took as a thank you.

'You're welcome, mate. Remember the carrots.' He picked one up and handed it to Ben, who accepted it with sauce-covered fingers.

Lucy had managed to get sauce on her bib, her face and in her hair.

Gabe laughed. 'Sweetheart, the sauce is for the sausage, or do you want to be eaten up too?'

She held out her chubby hands. 'More.'

He cut her another sausage, caught Rory surreptitiously dropping his capsicum off the side of the tray and coaxed him into eating it, and then rescued the sippy cup that Ben had decided to test for leaks by holding it upside down and shaking it. As they finished their food the noise levels rose again, especially when he opened the freezer. Squeals of delight rang through the kitchen as he scooped out ice cream into cones.

'Me!'

'My!'

'Num-num!'

'Ice cream's always a winner.' Gabe sprinkled hundreds and thousands on top of the cones as a holiday treat, although a small voice inside his head kept asking when his holiday was going to start.

When they're eighteen.

His day-to-day routine wasn't very different down here from what it was in Melbourne, except he wasn't working.

You've been working with Elly.

Not today. He'd hated the jab of disappointment that had slugged him when she hadn't called into the vaccination clinic, although after last night he wasn't sure where they stood with each other. Their past hurts and dented dreams circled them like living, breathing beings, impinging on everything they thought and said; making being together a minefield of unexploded bombs.

He handed out the ice creams and watched the kids virtually inhale them. Even though the triplets had been eating real food for months, he was still amazed at how much food ended up all over them as well as in them. 'Bathtime soon.'

The doorbell pealed. Why did people always call in at 'arsenic hour'? It was probably one of his parents' friends calling in for a 'happy hour' drink. Perhaps he could shanghai them to help him with bathtime. *Yeah, right.* Checking that the children were securely strapped in and busily occupied eating their favourite food, he left the kitchen and opened the front door. For a moment he just stared.

'Hello, Gabe.'

Elly stood on his parents' front veranda wearing a short pin-tucked sleeveless sundress, the vivid watermelon colour making her chestnut bob gleam and her eyes glow a deep, rainforest green. The dress showed off her long honey-brown arms and legs, immediately reminding him how they'd wrapped deliciously around his body the previous day, infusing him with energy and lust and making him feel instantly alive. *The most alive you've felt in two, long years.*

Women in my life equals disaster, remember, and Elly, like Jenna, is a case in point.

Nervous energy encircled her and she seemed to be looking beyond him, and into the house. She cleared her throat. 'Cathleen asked me to collect the Coast-Care gear for Saturday. Could you please tell her I'm here?'

'Coast-Care gear?' He knew he sounded inane but his brain was struggling to move from a haze of longing to deciphering why Elly was here now when his parents were in Hobart. 'Mum and Dad are in Hobart tonight.'

Elly paled. 'But your mother said—'

A scream and a cry sounded from inside, instantly grounding him. He hurried back to the kitchen, calling out 'Come in' as he went. He found Lucy leaning sideways, trying to grab Ben's ice cream with one hand and pushing her other one onto his face.

'Fair go, Luce, you've had your ice cream and that one's Ben's.'

He removed Lucy's hand and pulled Ben's highchair away, slightly increasing the space between them. Ben immediately howled his protest, reaching out for his sister, who a moment ago had been the last person on earth he wanted. Rory joined in by throwing his half-demolished cone at his sibling and Lucy shrieked her protest.

Somehow, above it all he heard the click-clack

of Elly's sandals on the tiled floor and he turned, throwing his arms out to encompass the chaos that was his life. 'Welcome to the madhouse.'

CHAPTER SIX

ELLY took in the tight grimace on Gabe's lips that had appeared when he'd first seen her, and the sight and sound of tired triplets.

My life is complicated, Elly.

He doesn't want you here so just get the stuff and leave. Now.

She had no clue why his mother had insisted she collect the gear tonight when Cathleen and James weren't even there, but with three screaming children, now wasn't the time to ask. 'Um, if you can just tell me where the Coast-Care stuff is, I'll get out of your way and leave you to it.'

Gabe picked up a damp face-washer and started to wipe sticky faces and hands, making soothing noises as he went. 'I think Dad put all fifteen boxes in the shed.'

'Fifteen?' She hadn't expected quite so much stuff.

The cries of the children reached fever pitch and her first instinct was to rush forward and help. She stomped on the feeling because even though Gabe's parents were in Hobart, surely he had Jenna. But no one else had appeared in the kitchen and the noise the triplets were making would raise the dead.

His blue eyes suddenly took on a familiar calculating gleam, the one that had always appeared when he'd had an idea he wanted to sell to her. 'Tell you what; if you give me a hand to get this crew sorted through the bath and into bed, I'll carry all the boxes out to your car.'

His request surprised her, eating into her resolve to leave. *Haul the gear yourself.* She glanced at the empty doorway. Where was his wife? 'There's no one else here to help you?'

He shook his head. 'Not tonight, no. Normally I wouldn't ask because I can do it all on my own but they're tired and will be beside themselves by the time I've finished. Believe me, that's no fun.'

In the past he would have beamed a flirting and beguiling smile—one that had once made her dizzy with longing and drained her brain of all common sense—and she'd capitulate and help. But that was a million years ago from now and the Gabe in front of her seemed barely able to generate a tired smile. The only emotion emanating from him was resigned fatigue.

He's got another life now, remember.

The children's cries were close to hysterical and they broke her resolve. *Sucker.* She immediately rejected the concept. She couldn't just walk away when he'd asked for help so she'd give him a hand and when the children were more settled she'd get the answers to her questions, and the Coast-Care boxes. 'OK, so what's the plan?'

'Can you run the bath and I'll wipe them clean enough to get to the bathroom without painting the walls with dinner? The bathroom's just up the hall on your left and I've set up the towels and pyjamas already.'

She tried not to look stunned as she struggled to align this epitome of organisation with the man who'd frequently got into the shower and then yelled for her to bring soap, towels or whatever else he'd forgotten. 'Sure, I can do that.'

'Thanks.'

The genuineness of his smile spun through her like sunshine after rain, doing delicious things to her. *You're just here to help and leave, remember. Help and leave.*

She found the bathroom easily and ran the bath-water, making sure it was the right temperature, and then she heard the thump of running feet. A moment later three toddlers burst into the room like a whirlwind and Elly found herself leaning back slightly in astonishment. She was used to dealing with one child at a time but this package of three did everything at full pelt.

'Ba-Ba.'

'Up, me.'

Lucy didn't bother with any words, just tried to sling one leg over the edge of the bath and climb straight in.

'Whoa, there, sweetie. Let's get your nappy off first.' Elly gently caught her around the middle, her palms connecting with warm, chubby flesh— an instant reminder of her own empty arms. With trembling fingers she undid the nappy before sitting the little girl in the water.

The blue-eyed child looked at her curiously but didn't object or cry.

'Right, you lot, bathtime.' Gabe walked in, barefooted and bare chested, and kneeled down next to her and the boys.

Elly's heart flipped as heat poured through her. Memories of laying her head on his chest and running her fingers over the toned flesh pounded her, and her hands cramped as she stopped them from reaching out to touch him. *He's not yours and he's out of bounds.* Had she known helping him was going to be this hard, she never would have agreed to help.

He whipped off the boys' nappies and lifted them into the bath to join their sister, his attention completely focused on the kids. 'This is Elly. Can you say Elly?'

Lucy's lips gave it a try. 'Lee.'

Elly smiled. 'That's close enough.'

Gabe flipped open some 'no tears' bath gel and shampoo and after putting some on his palm handed it to her with a smile. 'I'll wash Luce because she usually objects to her hair being washed so feel free to choose a boy.'

'Who is who?' The boys looked identical to her.

'Ben's on your left and Rory on your right. It's easy in the bath because Ben has a birth mark on his hip but in clothes they can trick me.'

Gabe leaned in over the bath, the muscles on his arms bunching as he washed his daughter's hair, and Elly had to force herself to look away. She smiled at one of the boys. 'Your turn, Ben.'

As she reached into the bath, Rory stood up with a plastic teapot and lifted it high. 'Grow you.'

Suddenly water cascaded over her hair and down the front of her dress and she gasped in surprise, then turned toward Gabe and laughed. 'I think I know why you took off your shirt.'

'Rory, you only water people when they're in the bath with you.' Gabe gently remonstrated with his son and removed the teapot.

'Sorry, Elly.' His husky words hung between them as he passed her a towel, his gaze zeroing in for a moment on her soaked dress, which now clung to her breasts like a second skin. His irises darkened to navy, instantly backlit with recollections of the time they'd dived fully clothed under a waterfall in Vanuatu and her T-shirt had become transparent.

His head rose and she met his gaze, which immediately blanked as if the memory meant nothing. He jerked his head away, fixing his attention on Lucy.

'No problem.' Her throat strangled her reply as she quickly scooped up the towel, pressing it against her chest. *Deep breaths.* But her brain betrayed her by reeling out in slow motion the vision of how he'd peeled off her clothes and made long, sweet love to her behind the falls in a private space created by a curtain of water.

The coolness in Gabe's eyes now made a mockery of her tingling breasts and the arrow of heat that had fired straight to the sensitive spot between her legs, making it quiver with need. *It isn't real need, it's just a reaction to a memory.*

Thankfully, the children's splashes and laughter and the fact they required washing, drying and dressing zoomed in, defusing her inappropriate feelings and giving her time to pull herself together. They worked together side by side, each of them talking to the children but not to each other.

Gabe marshalled the now pyjama-clad triplets in front of the closed door and Elly couldn't get over how different they looked after a bath— almost angelic.

He opened the door. 'And now for bed.'

'Book!' Lucy's eyes lit up.

'Nigh' nigh'.' Ben put his hands up to Gabe, as if to say, 'Pick me up.'

'Sing.' Rory ran from the bathroom.

Gabe picked up Ben and gave Elly a look that was half apologetic and half uncompromising. 'We've got this whole going-to-sleep routine.'

A slug of irrational hurt pinged her at the unspoken exclusion, which was ridiculous because she knew she was just a convenient pair of hands. He'd asked for help on his own terms and she had no connection to the children. In fact, her being in the room would probably prevent them from settling. 'I'll tidy up here but as soon as you've finished I really need to get those boxes so I can head home.'

'I haven't forgotten.' His expression was prosaic,

as if her request was just another thing he had to do in a long list of jobs. As he was leaving the room he pulled a towelling robe off the back of the door and, without looking at her, shoved it toward her. 'Wear this while your dress dries.'

She didn't want to wear his robe but she knew she couldn't keep wearing the dress so she reluctantly accepted. As he left she closed the door behind him and stripped off the sopping garment. She slipped her arms into the robe, and Gabe's scent of fresh soap and spices enveloped her. Dropping her face into the wide lapels, she breathed in deeply before looking up and catching her reflection, eyes dazed with lust and cheeks flushed pink with need.

Don't do this to yourself. Memories are overblown and he's not free. Even if he was, there's too much hurt between you.

She splashed her face with cold water, lassoed the robe's tie tightly around her waist so it didn't fall forward and expose her breasts and then she set about tidying up the bathroom, which looked like a tidal wave had hit it.

She could hear Gabe's deep and melodious

voice from the bathroom and she padded up the hall toward the bedroom, standing slightly back from the doorway. Gabe had his back to the door and the children lay in their cots, with 'cuddlies' under their arms, listening to him playing the guitar and singing.

The children were totally quiet, in stark contrast to the earlier uproar in the kitchen and the bathroom, and their heavy eyelids fluttered closed as the song continued. Elly didn't recognise the song or the tune and suddenly realised it was triplet specific. Gabe had written it just for his children.

The man you didn't trust enough to change his mind is the perfect father. Her heart ripped open at her own stupid mistakes.

Furious with herself, she stomped to the kitchen and started clearing up, taking her frustration out on the plastic plates as she jammed them into the dishwasher.

'What's the problem, El?'

She swung around at the quietly spoken words to find Gabe—an old, soft cotton T-shirt gracing his chest—standing quietly looking at her, concern clear on his handsome face.

Once she would have walked into his arms and told him everything but that wasn't available to her any more. Besides, she didn't want his concern or understanding pouring salt into her self-created wounds. She jammed in another plate. 'What's going on, Gabe? Your mother specifically told me to come after six tonight and I turn up to find you're the only person here.'

'Yeah, I'm just as surprised about that as you are.' He strode to the fridge and grabbed a long, green bottle of wine from the door, spun the cap and broke the seal. For a moment the only sound was the straw-coloured liquid glugging into glasses. 'I think we've both been Cathleened.'

'Excuse me?'

He sighed. 'I think my mother got you over here to help me with the kids.'

Elly took a big sip of wine. 'Why would she do that?'

His shoulders rose and fell. 'She's picked up that there's been something between us and in her own misguided way she was trying to help.'

Elly stared at him slack-mouthed. 'But you're married! And *been* infers the past and over.' She pushed her hair behind her ears, tugging it hard as if that would help her understand. 'How could she even think that your wife would be happy about an ex-girlfriend helping out with her children?'

Gabe closed his eyes for a moment and drew in a long, deep breath before raising a troubled gaze to hers. 'Because I'm a widower, Elly.'

The wineglass slipped from her suddenly numb fingers as her blood drained to her feet. Of all the possible answers he could have given, she hadn't expected that. 'Jenna's dead?' The thoughtless words slipped out as she tried wrapping her brain around the information that he didn't have a wife and, tragically, those gorgeous little children didn't have a mother. 'I thought she…' She swallowed the rest of her sentence.

'You thought what?'

Her brain wouldn't cough up anything to cover the uncomfortable moment as his gaze bored into her. 'I thought she was here with you and the children.'

His face suddenly darkened like clouds before a

storm. 'You thought I was married, even though we kissed each other senseless? Hell, Elly, it's good to know you've got such a high opinion of me.'

I was single when I met Jenna. Oh, God, she'd done it again and jumped to conclusions. 'I'm sorry.' Guilt fluttered against the wall of her stomach. 'But in my defence, you said the kiss was a mistake and you told me your life was complicated.'

'It *was* a mistake and of course my life is complicated!' He grabbed the toppled glass, mumbling something about mistakes before picking up a cloth to soak up the spilled wine. 'I'm a single father of three and barely keeping everything together.'

And a grieving widower. Elly watched him pour her more wine, suddenly seeing him through different lenses. The new lines on his face and the strain around his eyes she'd put down to exhaustion, but now she knew it was much more than that. His handsome face bore the scars of someone who'd been through an emotional wringer. The mother of his children was dead. The woman he'd loved was dead yet all she'd been able to do was think about how that impacted on her. Again.

Remorse flowed through her and she bit her lip. 'I've really stuffed up, haven't I? You wanted to tell me everything last night and I just went ballistic on you.'

'Pretty much.' He walked over to a leather sofa and sat down, an aura of resigned distance emanating from him. Distance she'd put there.

'And now?' She sat down next to him, respecting his emotional reserve by giving him physical space. Space she hated.

'Now what?' He sounded tired and flat.

She blew out a long breath, knowing her behaviour had made a traumatic event even harder on him, and decided right there and then that no matter how much she wanted to hammer him with questions, she had to hold back so he could tell it his way. It would be the hardest thing she'd ever had to do. 'Is it too late for me to listen?'

Gabe rubbed his face with his free hand, feeling the stubble rough against his palm. He finally had Elly in the right frame of mind to hear the story and a quiet and uninterrupted time and place to tell it, but doubts still lingered. 'It's not an easy story to hear, El.'

Her shoulders stiffened slightly, before rolling back in quiet determination. 'Then I doubt it will be easy to tell.'

She was right about that. *Just start.* 'Jenna died when the triplets were nine months old.'

She laced her fingers together. 'That must have been really tough for you all.'

'Tough. Yeah, you could say that.' He drained his wineglass, thinking how the word didn't even come close to describing the reality of the last two years. 'Actually, it was way worse than tough.'

'Losing a loved one is never easy.'

His head snapped up. Had he heard her right? If he'd been a patient, the Elly he knew would have reached out and touched his hand or gently squeezed his arm, but right now she sounded like a bereavement card and the words chafed against his shame for the entire debacle that had been Jenna and him.

Tell it fast. 'I met Jenna at a base jump. She was wild and fun, and out for a good time.' He shot her a look, wary of how she'd receive his next statement. 'I needed that after everything that had gone down between us.'

She nodded, her plump and kissable lips pressed together hard. 'I imagine you would have.'

What? Her words sat like lead in his chest. Of all the things she might have said, he hadn't expected that, but she was looking at him with an encouraging, although tight expression. He pushed on. 'Jenna was up for anything and I was up for escape.' He recalled how he'd taken massive risks with Jenna, unlike anything he'd ever done before, just to try and get Elly out of his system. 'But the morning I found Jenna and I twenty-five stories up and about to jump between two buildings where I knew the distance was further than we could safely jump was the day my eyes opened. What I'd initially thought was a vivacious "let's do it" personality was actually the start of her entering a manic phase of bipolar disorder.'

'We both know how hard bipolar is to diagnose in the early stages and hindsight is of little value, especially as she wasn't your patient.'

He tugged at his hair. 'And this was the classic situation. I had no clue she'd gone off the Pill or tampered with condoms and by the time I'd worked it all out, she was flying out of control and pregnant.'

A thousand questions stormed Elly's amazing eyes, but all she said in a very controlled voice was, 'That would have been a difficult situation for you both.'

Irritation fizzed through him as he recognised the reflective listening technique of an impartial counsellor: one who seemed to have taken the place of the passionate woman he knew normally wore her heart on her sleeve.

He gritted his teeth, feeling betrayed by her attitude. 'No, Elly, it wasn't difficult, it was bloody horrendous. Medication in pregnancy is fraught with dangers and Jenna refused to take anything. At seven weeks she was really ill with morning sickness and that's when we found out about the triplets.'

Elly bit her lip. 'Multiples can happen with post-Pill ovulation.'

'And don't I just know it.' He drank more wine.

'Jenna was thirty-three, her mother had been a twin, and with conceiving just off the Pill we got the trifecta, although my boys are identical twins, so that was just good luck.' He sighed. 'She was excited for about three days and agreed to be hospitalised and monitored, but then she started to come down from her manic phase and she took to absconding and disappearing for days at a time.'

He ran his hand through his hair, hating the rush of old emotions that surged through him, taking him back to that time when his carefree life had spiralled out of control and vanished forever, all because of *one* error in judgement. 'There was a period in the second trimester when Jenna was very settled and she started nesting and decorating the nursery. Despite the fact the pregnancy was not only unexpected but multiple, that I was going to be an instant father of three, and my wife was walking a health tightrope every single day, I had my own delusions during that time that everything would turn out OK.'

'You needed to believe that.'

Her softly spoken words mirrored his feelings

exactly, exacerbating his guilt and shame that he'd dropped his guard, partied hard and so many lives had been affected as a result. He raged against the feeling. 'You think? Well, you won't be surprised to know that it was all wishful thinking because when the triplets arrived, Jenna completely unravelled.'

Elly sat perfectly still except for a flutter of a pulse at the base of her throat. 'The arrival of triplets would stress even the most mentally fit person, and with Jenna's diagnosis, the puerperal period is particularly fraught with danger.'

What the hell? His exasperation at her manner spread like a hot, prickly rash and then burst into anger. How could she just sit there impassively, as if they were discussing a case history rather than his life?

'Elly, I'm well aware of how stressful having triplets is because that's *my* life. I love them to bits but every day is like working in a child-care centre.' He stood up, needing to move. 'As you so aptly described, Jenna spiralled into a puerperal psychosis after their arrival and was in and out of hospital. When she was home I had every support mechanism in the book to help us.'

'I'm sure you did everything possible.'

'It wasn't enough.' The words came out through gritted teeth. He wanted to yell, he wanted to put his fist through the wall, but more than anything he wanted to shake some reaction out of her un-naturally stiff and emotion-free responses. 'Jenna took her own life and as tragic as it was, it's made our life easier.'

She blinked in shock as his words registered and her mouth fell open.

Yes! Finally, she was going to say what she really thought.

She took in a deep breath. 'I imagine on one level things are easier but in many other ways they're harder.'

A cold fury overtook his fire of anger. 'For God's sake, Elly, cut it out.'

'What?' Behind the confusion he caught a glimpse of real emotions spinning in her eyes.

'I'm not your patient.'

'I *know* that.'

'Then what the hell is all this rubbish you're spouting?'

She stood up, throwing her arms out wide, and he caught a glimpse of gingham and lace before she pulled the robe tightly closed in a gesture that said, *Out of bounds to you, mate.*

'You're impossible to please, Gabe. Yesterday you told me I never listened and now that I have, that's wrong too. What do you want me to say? That I hate the thought that you knocked up a woman weeks after we separated? That you're a father and I'm not a mother?'

'Well, that's a given. I got that yesterday. But I've just told you about the worst time in my life and call me stupid, but I expected some empathy.'

Her bare feet slapped the floorboards. 'You didn't hear my empathy? Are you deaf? How could you have missed that I think the whole situation is tragic for everyone involved and will be for a long time to come?'

She pulled her hair back from her face, her expression so full of understanding that he thought he would suffocate from the guilt-ridden pain that surged through him in an unrelenting wave.

'Honour Jenna's memory through the children, Gabe, and they'll get you through.'

He fought against the black pit of despair that had hovered over him since Jenna's death. 'Don't patronise me.'

Shock jolted her but then her eyes flared with crystal-clear understanding and for the first time he felt seriously exposed, as if she'd just seen clear down to his soul.

'Are you after empathy or forgiveness, Gabe?'

The quietly spoken words streaked home and he spun away from her.

She gasped. 'Oh, my God, you want me to give you absolution. You want me to pat you on the arm and say, "Poor Gabe, you really got yourself into a pickle and it's been horrible but everything's going to be all right now and nothing was your fault."'

Her words burned into his shame and culpability with pinpoint accuracy and he turned back to her, defiant and attacking. 'That is the dumbest thing you've said all night.'

Elly nodded slowly. 'Yes, you're right.'

A trickle of relief dripped through his veins that she hadn't got close to his locked-down feelings about Jenna, his never-ending self-blame that he hadn't loved her and perhaps if he had she'd still be there to enjoy her wonderful children. 'I'm glad you can see that.'

'I can, because what I said wasn't quite on the money, was it? You don't need my forgiveness at all, Gabe, you need it from yourself.'

Blood roared in his ears as the walls seemed to close in on him. He wanted out. 'You don't have a clue what you're talking about, Elly.' He strode out of the side door toward the garage without waiting for a reply.

CHAPTER SEVEN

ELLY should have been thrilled at the turnout for the Coast-Care clean-up. The beach, the dunes and the park were dotted with people in bright, baggy T-shirts, all wearing gloves and clutching big, grey rubbish bags. Locals, holiday-house owners and tourists all mixed in together with *esprit de corps* as they went about trying to minimise their global footprint.

However, throughout the morning as she'd handed out gear, ticked off names and weighed rubbish, Elly kept thinking about Gabe, Jenna and the triplets. The story of the last two years was simply awful for all of them, and Gabe wore his guilt about Jenna like a suit of armour. Part of her understood his guilt—one decision had changed his life for ever and no matter how he'd tried to make amends and had done the right thing, Jenna had still died.

But another part of her—the bruised and reeling part—was totally frustrated with him. No matter what she did or said, it was wrong. They clashed every time they met and although she had a dangerous urge to try and help him work through his grief and pain, she decided that their shared past would prevent that from ever happening.

You helped him last night. But hands-on help with the cute triplets, although hectic, was the easy way to help. It was the emotional stuff overlaid with their past that was fraught with danger.

Ironically, Cathleen and James had made it to the clean-up after all, full of apologies about not being home when she'd visited.

'Jenny and Ian Gilbert couldn't use their symphony tickets so we decided at the last minute to go. At least Gabe was able to help with the boxes.' Cathleen had given her an open smile.

'Yes, he was most helpful.' As she'd directed them to their allocated section of the beach, she hadn't mentioned that he'd loaded her car in silent fury and had turned away the moment he'd slammed her tailgate shut. She hadn't seen him since.

'Hey, Doc.' Two teenage boys, their sleep-rumpled hair wild around their heads, smiled at her. 'Can we still help?'

'Absolutely.' Glad to be taken out of her reverie, and happy to be busy again, she organised the boys, who were the first crew of a new wave of volunteers streaming in to take over from the early birds. As the sun marched up to its zenith, the pile of rubbish bags on the trailer grew and by noon most people had finished and Elly was totalling up final figures.

'We might be more of a hindrance than a help with clean-up so we brought a thank-you picnic lunch instead.'

The familiar mellow voice washed over her bent head, entering her body on a slow stream of heat. Heat that moved through her, lighting fires of longing—fires she needed to douse because they would only taunt her with what might have been but now never could be.

She slowly raised her head, giving herself time to cover her feelings, although she knew her warm cheeks would betray her. Gabe stood in front of the trestle table, holding a boy in each arm. Lucy bounced in a backpack on his shoulders. Her heart tore a little more, as it did every time she saw him with his children—a constant reminder of what she didn't have. Given the massive elephant in the room that was their past, which dominated every meeting, she wasn't sure she could sit down to lunch with him or why, after the other night, he even wanted to. 'What are you thanking me for?'

'Your help with bathing the kids.'

She clipped pages onto her red clipboard with a snap. 'You loaded my car so we're even and a thank-you lunch really isn't necessary.'

'But I didn't exactly do my share of the deal with the same generous spirit you did.' His sky-blue eyes flickered across her face, apology shining brightly in their depths.

Lucy's small arms waved at her. 'Lee, Lee.'

Ben—or was it Rory?—leaned out of Gabe's arms toward her. 'Dig sand.'

Deep inside her a primal instinct stirred.

Not a good idea. But every part of her was

being pulled toward the idea of lunch by the children.

Gabe's eyes twinkled. 'Now, how could you possibly refuse an invitation so enthusiastically given?'

Just treat it as lunch with an acquaintance. Leave the elephant alone. 'Is there cake?'

'Lemon poppy-seed.'

The elephant trumpeted, *He remembered your favourite cake. No, it's his favourite cake,* and she pushed the elephant back where it belonged. 'Let's eat, then.'

Gabe had set up the picnic on a large rug under a shade awning. He sat the boys in the double stroller and then with a practised swing he safely took the backpack off his back with Lucy still in it, and set it up on the sand like a chair. He gave each child a cheese stick for one hand and a celery stick for the other.

She watched him, still struggling with how organised he'd become and how he seemed to do everything with a self-containment she'd never noticed in other fathers. All too often they hand-balled parenting duties to their wives but Gabe didn't have that luxury and it sounded like he'd never had it. He'd been the hands-on parent from the start and the bond he'd forged with his children seemed almost exclusive.

He sat down next to her and smiled, a quiet but devastating twitch of his lips that raced through golden stubble, around his ever-present fatigue and up into his eyes like the dazzling white of a sparkler.

Her self-imposed calm shattered, her breathing suddenly shortened and she forced air down deep into her lungs. *Lunch was a dumb idea.*

He pulled two plastic containers from the cooler and she recognised the familiar logo of the newly opened Midden Cove Café and Caterers. He ripped off the lids and handed one to her. Moist, cold chicken nestled against a green salad and the aroma of garlic and lemon made her stomach rumble. 'This looks fantastic.'

He grinned. 'Great. You take your time to savour it but I'm eating fast because I reckon I've got fifteen minutes before they're going to want to be in the water.'

She could just imagine one of the triplets

running off in the opposite direction of the other two or possibly all three running off in different directions. 'Won't you need more than just you to supervise them?'

He nodded. 'Mum and Dad are going to come back down.'

She accepted the proffered cutlery, glad to be thinking about the logistics of outings with the triplets as a way of keeping things between them more normal instead of fraught with the battle-field of emotions that had characterised their other encounters. 'How do you manage work and the kids back in Melbourne?'

He opened a bottle of cold water. 'It's something that's always changing but currently I'm doing four twelve-hour days a week in A and E, and having three days off in a row.'

No wonder he looked exhausted. 'Are they in child care when you're at work?' She thought they might be, given how easily they'd coped with her presence at bathtime.

He shook his head. 'I've got two great nannies that cover the days I'm at work so the kids can stay at home. They do the evening routine of dinner and baths and, emergencies excepted, I'm always home for bedtime.'

She remembered the song he'd sung to the triplets and suddenly understood why he'd been determined to put them to bed on his own. 'That's your special time with them, isn't it?'

His face lightened with a look of appreciation. 'After the turmoil of their first nine months, I've tried to give them as much stability as I can, which is why we're on holidays now.'

'Stability—I don't quite get how that's related to this holiday.'

'Both Bella and Lauren, the nannies, are in their twenties and have boyfriends who are keen surfers. They wanted to be off for the month so I took leave and came down here.'

She stared at the calm ocean. 'Well, Midden Cove is an ideal holiday place.'

'Daddy.'

The cheese sticks had been eaten and the celery gnawed, and the triplets started babbling and pointing. Gabe quickly opened another container. 'Here it comes.' He held the container aloft and pretended to fly it toward the children.

'Me.'

'Mine.'

They clapped their hands in delight as he let each of them choose their own slice of watermelon and Elly had to work hard at not feeling like she was an outsider looking in on a four-way partnership. 'They're totally full on, aren't they?'

He fell back onto the rug. The new lines cut in deeply around his eyes but the laughter lines around his mouth softened the look. 'They pretty much go from dawn till dusk, like that bunny they use to advertise batteries. Most days they have an afternoon sleep and because we're on holidays, I usually have one too.'

She stared down at him, trying not to let the past hover but without success. 'I can't imagine you ever needing a nap.'

'Things change, El, life changes us. Once my life was bookended by adventures and beautiful women like you. Now my life is bookended by work and the triplets and I don't see that changing.' He sighed. 'I can't even finish conversations.

Sorry, what were we talking about before the kids interrupted?'

She tried to think back and concentrate but her brain has stalled on 'beautiful'. 'Um, that Midden Cove is a great place for a holiday.'

'It is, but you're not here for holidays.' He shot her a quizzical look. 'Are you in Midden Cove for someone, El?'

The question came out of left field and she breathed in far too quickly, shooting a piece of chicken into her throat. She started coughing and gasping for air simultaneously, and tears streamed down her face.

Gabe dropped his lunch box and immediately thumped her firmly on the back twice as she coughed and finally dislodged the meat.

'Here, drink this.'

He handed her the water bottle and she gulped down the contents before wiping her face with the back of her hand.

He silently handed her a napkin and watched her, his eyes glinting with an unusual hint of silver in them. 'I'm taking nearly choking on that question as a yes, then. It's that bloke who picked you up the other day, isn't it?'

No. She tugged her hair behind her ears. 'Dev's a…' She paused for a moment, wondering exactly how to define him. *That alone is telling.* 'He's a friend.'

A ripple of tension hovered around him. 'He doesn't look at you like he's a friend.'

She pulled at a chicken wing. 'Of course he does.'

'No, Elly, he looks at you like you're *his*.'

The tone in his voice made her heart give a traitorous hiccough. Did he have any feelings left for her after all this time? 'Does that bother you?'

His jaw tightened so much it threatened to snap. 'Elly, you left me to find someone and I've had two years to get used to that idea, but as someone who was in a nightmare of a marriage, something I am *never* going to repeat, all I can say to you is make sure this guy is the one.'

Work and the triplets and I don't see that changing.

That was why he was so self-contained with the triplets.

The kiss was a mistake.

A mistake because he didn't want a relationship with anyone. Her heart ached despite itself.

Why? You've both hurt each other too much. You know it would never work out so put your big-girl pants on!

It's not about me, I'm just sad for him and the triplets.

He reached out his hand and the tips of his fingers barely brushed her cheek with the softest touch before falling to his side. 'I'm in Midden Cove for a few weeks and it seems a waste to spend that time stuck in the mire of our past. I know we've hurt each other but do you think there's any possibility we can move round everything that's happened and find a way to be friends?'

Friends? Her cheek burned from his touch as the banked heat inside sent flames licking at every part of her. Even in the biggest denial room of her heart she knew that the touch of a friend wouldn't send delicious tingles through her or make her want to pull him against her so his body lined hers.

But there was no ambiguity in what Gabe had said. He only wanted friendship. Most of her knew he was right—a future as a couple when they only seemed to inflict hurt on each other wasn't going to work. But friends?

A traitorous sea of sadness pooled inside her and her brain seized under all the conflicting emotions so all she could get out was, 'You want us to try to be friends?'

'You're right, it's an idea riddled with quicksand and probably way too hard.' He sat up, running his hand through his hair, and his eyes held a haunting desolation. 'What if I threw in the odd hospital shift and we settled for colleagues?'

She bit her lip, needing the sharp pain to stop herself from throwing her arms around him and kissing him until the desolation vanished. 'No. Yes. I mean yes to both. I can use a hand occasionally and although it's probably going to be rocky, I think you're right. Friendship is our only option.'

'So it's a deal?' A myriad of undecipherable

emotions swirled in his eyes as he held out his hand.

She stared at his broad, tanned hand with its long, tapered fingers; fingers that in the past had soothed her, stroked her, caressed her, and brought her to ecstasy. Not once had they ever wrapped themselves around her hand in a perfunctory handshake.

You just agreed to friendship and this is what it is.

'Dig!'

'Out, me, *now!*' Lucy held up her arms.

'Jubba, jubba.'

Elly spun round to the children, thankful for the distraction, and she bobbed down in front of Lucy. Reaching in, she unclipped the safety strap before the little girl knocked the backpack over. 'Time for a paddle.'

'Up.' Lucy held her arms out to her.

Delight streaked through her confused and battered heart. She lifted the little girl high into the air and spun her around like a plane before running down to the water, never more glad to have an excuse to put some distance between her and Gabe. This friendship was going to be the hardest one she'd ever had.

'How's it all going?'

Elly's voice came down the phone line and the image of her teeth pulling at her plump, cherry-red bottom lip socked into Gabe. His groin immediately tightened and he blew out a long, slow breath, thankful that at least he couldn't smell her ocean-fresh perfume because that always made his blood run hot. He knew lusting after a friend was bad and, so help him, he didn't want to crave her with every fibre of his being, but every time he thought he'd got his newly returned libido under control, his body would laugh in his face.

Just a*ct like a friend*. 'Not much is going on at all.' Elly had gone to Hobart for a meeting and Gabe had offered to be on call. 'In fact, I'm finishing up a very quiet afternoon clinic where the most exciting thing that happened was that Manny Abraham stuck a currant up both nostrils at playgroup.'

'Again?' She laughed. 'Poor Ruth. Two weeks ago he put sultanas in his ears.'

'I did suggest that he not be given any foods smaller than a biscuit.' He swung around in his chair and gazed out the window toward the road. 'So, where are you?'

Careful, you're sounding like you care what time she gets back.

No! A friend can ask a question like that.

It had been a week since he'd suggested they try being friends. After the emotional quicksand of the first few days after he'd met Elly again, friendship had seemed like the only solution available to them. He needed a way to move forward too because he and Jenna had been a nightmare, and he and Elly had burned each other so badly that starting over as a couple wasn't an option. Besides, the thought of another relationship with all its inherent pitfalls and heartache made him shudder. Yet despite knowing all that, he just wasn't ready to say goodbye to Elly completely.

So far the friendship attempt had seemed strained but with moments of relaxation; like the other day when Elly and the boys had lost their balance jumping tiny waves and with gales of laughter had pulled him and Lucy into the water with them. It was times like that which gave him a glimmer of hope that they could actually pull this friendship off. Right then he realised with a start that the few times they'd got together, it had always involved time with the triplets, and the two of them had never been alone.

Elly's voice bounced enthusiastically down the line. 'I'm twenty minutes away. Do you want to get together—?'

The phone crackled, cutting off her words. *Just the two of us for dinner? Sure. For a drink? Absolutely.* 'Sorry, El, you broke up and I missed that.'

'It's low tide and as it's still early I thought the triplets might enjoy a rock-pool ramble. That is, if one or both of your parents are able to come too so we can have one on one and not lose anyone.'

Disappointment rammed him hard in the gut, sparking an immediate spurt of frustration directed at himself. *Fledgling friendship is the only thing you and El can handle. That doesn't include dating.*

'Gabe? Or isn't it a good idea?'

The hesitancy in her voice underpinned how both of them were stepping on eggshells around each other. He forced himself to sound enthusiastic. 'It's a great idea.'

'Excellent. Let's meet at Bluff Point in half an hour and bring their beach buckets.'

'Three hats, check, three sunscreened kids, check.'

Gabe had the children lined up and ready on the sandy beach at Bluff Point.

'Bucket, dig me?' Rory asked as he swung the bucket around.

'Not digging, mate, but we're looking at starfish.'

'Twinkle, twinkle, star.'

Lucy wiggled her pudgy fingers and Gabe laughed.

A hat suddenly got pushed onto his head. 'One hat for the father.' His mother smiled at him. 'This is a lovely idea of Elly's.'

'Mum.' He gave a look that he knew quelled junior residents. He'd already spoken to his mother about asking Elly to collect the boxes, but she'd sworn black and blue that the Gilberts had only offered the concert tickets after she'd made the arrangement, and in the rush to get to Hobart on time she'd completely forgotten. 'Don't get any ideas about Elly and me. There's too much history and right now we're struggling just to be friends.'

Cathleen's brows rose in surprise. 'Trying to be friends is…' She seemed to consider her thoughts. 'It's admirable, darling, although I'd have thought it fraught with difficulties. All I meant was this outing is a nice idea of Elly's and a good opportunity for her to practise as a volunteer rambling guide.' She patted her sunhat into position.

Gabe had the distinct impression he'd just given away more than he should have. A general wave of dissatisfaction washed through him but he wasn't sure if it was due to his mother's comments about the problem of ex-lovers trying to be friends or the fact that Elly's motives for the outing weren't all about spending time with him. 'What's a rambling guide?'

'Haven't you wondered why your father's been reading all about the local marine life? He and Elly are trainee ramblers as part of the upcoming school holiday programme.' She laughed and gave a wave as Elly appeared at the top of the stairway. 'Although the triplets are not going to give them any tough questions so we'll have to do that.'

Behind his sunglasses, Gabe watched Elly descend the stairs to the beach, her feet clad in reef-shoes and her long, shapely legs exposed from mid-thigh by cut-off jeans, but it was the movement of her old T-shirt that riveted his attention. It rose and fell seductively, exposing a band of tanned midriff along with a sparkling gem belly-button stud. Heat poured through him and he tore his gaze away, wishing he could dive into the cold surf to cool down and find perspective.

Sex with Elly is a seriously bad idea.

Really? His lust-filled body disagreed loudly. *It's been so long since I had sex.*

Then find someone else.

The idea lacked appeal.

Elly walked over to them, her wide smile dancing around his family group. 'Hi, James, Cathleen.' A ripple of tension shot across her shoulders. 'Gabe.'

'Hey, Elly.' He hated the tension that always hovered between them and wondered if it would ever fade.

She tucked her hair behind her ears. 'James, I'm hoping you can help me with my cnidarians.'

His father laughed. 'I'll trade you cnidarians for ascidians.'

Envy bit him at the easy camaraderie that flowed between his father and Elly, which was in stark contrast to the strained atmosphere he and Elly shared. 'Who knew you two would bond over anemones and sea squirts?' The statement came out overly curt.

Surprise raced across Elly's cheeks but she didn't reply, and instead patted the triplets on their red-hatted heads. 'Are you lobsters ready for an adventure?'

'Buck.' Ben smiled at his new word as he held up his bucket.

'Go Lee.' Lucy pointed to herself.

Rory just tugged on James's hand as if to ask if they couldn't just start.

'Let's go, then.' Elly held Lucy's hand and started the short walk to the exposed basalt and sandstone reef.

James and Rory followed and his mother scooped up Ben. Gabe found himself walking behind, experiencing one of the few occasions, aside from work, when he didn't have a child in his arms or hanging off his hand. It should have been liberating; instead if felt strangely like he was the stranger in this excursion and his parents had a connection with Elly he couldn't seem to grasp.

Another family was wandering around on the reef, gazing into the rock pools. Two boys, who looked to be about ten and twelve, charged ahead, putting distance between them and their parents. 'Be careful,' their mother called to their retreating backs.

Elly watched the boys running off, and her brow creased in a slight frown.

'Something wrong?' Gabe asked quietly.

She moved her head back and forth as she shrugged her shoulders, the motion vacillating. 'Not really, I guess. It's just if they were mine, I'd be keeping them closer.' Elly squatted down in front of the triplets. 'We have to hold hands when we're looking in the water and you can only touch what I put in your bucket, OK?'

The triplets nodded in response to the serious tone in her voice.

'Fish.' Rory hopefully held out his bucket.

'I think the fish might be a bit fast for me to catch but I can show you something else.' Elly took his bucket and put it into the pool for a moment and then handed it back to him.

Gabe looked at the beautiful five-armed, orange star. 'Hey, Rory, Elly's found you a starfish.'

'Actually, it's a biscuit star.' James helped Rory put the sea-star on his fingers, all the while keeping it underwater.

'Num-nums?' Rory looked confused.

'It's not that sort of biscuit.'

Gabe and Elly's words laughingly tumbled over each other in a blend of harmonies that instantly recalled the past. The good past when they'd had simpatico, something he now realised he missed.

He found himself grinning at her as a bubble of happiness floated through him, a sign that perhaps they could find a friendship groove after all. 'So remind me, what's its real name?'

'It's an echinoderm and look…' she put a sea-star in Ben and Lucy's buckets before turning one over to show the children '…they eat through this hole.'

'More?' Lucy peered into the water.

James took Rory to another pool as Elly put her hand back in and picked up a hermit crab. 'He takes his house with him.' The bright orange creature with blue eyes quickly retreated into its current shell.

'Hey, Elly, I've found an elephant snail.' James sounded as if he'd just won the lottery.

Cathleen shuddered as she walked Ben and Lucy over. 'James, I really don't know how you can stick your hands in these pools.'

'That's why we did the training, sweetheart, so we know what *not* to pick up.'

Elly moved to stand up and Gabe automatically

extended his hand to help her. Her palm hit his with seductive softness and the urge to pull her up and into his arms roared through him like a hot north wind. She quickly dropped his hand the moment she was upright and immediately looked toward his parents and the triplets.

It was the first time they'd been alone and he wanted to extend the moment. His eyes lit on the pale green-and-yellow plant that seemed to dominate the area. 'I've always wondered what this is called.'

'Oh, that's an easy one.' With dancing eyes, Elly scooped up a few strands of the wet and dripping plant and draped it around his neck. 'Neptune's necklace.'

Her perfume and energy circled him, pulling at every resolution he'd made about her, mocking his attempt to keep her at a distance by trying to be friends. 'Not Salacia's strands?' He swung some of the plant around her neck, remembering the time he'd given her a gold chain necklace for her birthday. 'All wise men know it's the woman who gets the jewellery.'

She stilled as the memory passed between them.

'Perhaps that's why Salacia hid from Neptune, because of his penchant for necklaces.'

He stroked the stray stands of hair from her cheek, tucking them behind her ear like she often did. 'Nah, she was in awe of him and rode back to him on a dolphin.'

The green of her eyes disappeared under a disc of wide black and the tip of her tongue touched her plump top lip before she swallowed hard. 'I've always had a soft spot for dolphins.'

In a primal rush of need that consumed every part of him, he stared into her eyes. *She feels it too.* He wanted to pull her close, feel her breasts flatten against his chest, have her long legs pressed hard against his own, and fill her mouth with his. He wanted to taste her, have her heat ignite his and lose himself in the mind-blowing sensations he'd always experienced when he'd kissed her.

'Elly.' Her name came out on a croak of need combined with utter frustration that they really weren't alone at all, and to do anything would expose them as much as the reef they were standing on.

'Mum!'

The terrified shriek of a boy curdled his blood.

'Jack's been bitten by a blue-ring.'

Elly turned and ran.

CHAPTER EIGHT

'WHAT can we do?' Shock and fear lined James's face.

'Get the kids off the reef and call an ambulance.'

Gabe raced after Elly, who'd pulled off her T-shirt, and by the time he reached her, she was shredding it into strips.

'I'm a doctor, Jack, and you must lie perfectly still.' Elly instructed the boy as she laid him down.

'I'm Gabe and I'm a doctor too. Are you sure it was a blue-ringed octopus? I didn't think they'd be in Tassie.'

'We get them here.' Elly bit the material with her mouth.

The younger boy nodded. 'I saw the bright blue rings and told him to drop it.'

'It's too late to do anything once you see the

rings.' Elly started wrapping the boy's arm with the strips of her T-shirt, making a compression bandage.

The boys' parents arrived out of breath from running, their faces white with shock. 'Do you know what you're doing?' The father stared at Elly's halter bikini top and sparkling belly-button ring and immediately moved forward, his actions pure protection.

Gabe put his hand on the man's shoulder. 'She's slowing down the spread of the venom. We're both doctors and she certainly knows what she's doing.'

'Oh, like snakebite.' The mother nodded her understanding. 'So there'll be antivenin at the hospital?'

Elly's hands kept bandaging but her gaze hit Gabe's with the message to tell them because she couldn't waste precious seconds.

There was no easy way to give this news. 'I'm afraid there's no antivenin for blue-ring octopus bites.'

'Oh, God, what does that mean?' Jack's mother gripped his arm.

'I feel sick,' moaned Jack.

Elly tied a knot in the bandage that now covered the length of Jack's arm. 'Gabe, we need to get off the reef. Pick him up and run.' She stood and looked at the terrified parents. 'Follow us.'

Elly's bullet-point instructions rammed home the critical situation and Gabe scooped up the boy, moving as fast as he could, given he was picking his way across uneven, wet rocks and around large pools of water.

Elly ran alongside. 'Take him to the bottom of the stairs and we'll reassess before we attempt to get him to the car park.' She put her hand on the boy's head. 'Jack, can you see me?'

'You're fuzzy.' Fear laced the boy's words.

The venom was spreading and doing its damage. Gabe's feet finally hit sand and he tightened his grip on Jack and really ran. A long minute later he lowered the boy onto the sand. 'Can you squeeze my hand?' He put his palm into the unbitten hand.

Jack gave a feeble squeeze.

'Gabe, the ambulance is on the way and we're taking the triplets home.'

'Thanks, Dad.' Gabe nodded to his father and prayed the ambulance wasn't far away because he'd feel a lot happier with an air-viva and a tube to maintain Jack's airway when the inevitable happened.

'What's going to happen?' Shaking, Jack's mother fell to her knees next to her son.

Elly took her hand. 'Like Gabe said, we're going to do everything we can for Jack. Your job is to stay calm so Jack stays calm.'

The woman breathed in deeply, valiantly trying to find some semblance of composure. 'OK, but tell me what's going to happen.'

'We've tried to slow down the circulation of the toxin but his vision is blurred and he's nauseated so it's starting to spread, and eventually it will paralyse him.'

'Oh, God.' Sharon's hand covered her mouth as if trying to stop her fear.

'Jack can hear us and understand us, but he won't be able to speak and we're going to have to use a ventilator to breathe for him until the toxin wears off.' Elly continued to hold the woman's hand. 'I promise you, we're doing everything we can and he's in good hands.'

Gabe kept a close eye on Jack as he listened to Elly's words. He'd always admired the way she could empathise with patients, which was why he'd been so gutted the night he'd told her about Jenna. He'd expected more. Needed more.

You just hated it that she was right. You loathe what you did to Jenna and if you hadn't been using sex to forget Elly you might have seen the real and struggling Jenna.

But he hadn't seen it. He'd missed all the tell-tale signs and that ate into him more than anything.

We both know how hard bipolar is to diagnose in the early stages and hindsight is of little value, especially as she wasn't your patient.

Elly's words kept coming back to him. On one level he knew she was right. He and Jenna had been consenting adults—out for fun, good times and no commitment, although he knew now that was an oxymoron. But on the other hand he just couldn't get past the fact that if he'd realised earlier that she was sick, things would have been very different.

But then you wouldn't have the triplets.

The thought both shocked and steadied him. Being a father was the most challenging thing he'd ever done and even though he was constantly exhausted and had no desire for any more children, he couldn't imagine his life without Rory, Ben and Lucy.

Honour Jenna's memory through the children. Was that the key to putting his demons to rest? But how the hell did he do that?

'We love you, mate.' Jack's father's gruff tones said it all as he flanked his son. 'How's his breathing, Doc?'

Gabe had been resting his hand lightly on Jack's chest, monitoring his breathing, and could now feel his increasingly shallow respirations. 'Not so good.' Where the hell was the ambulance? 'Jack, I might have to give you mouth-to-mouth soon, but it'll be OK, I promise.'

The boy's pupils—fixed, dilated and stark with fear—stared blindly at him as the toxin-generated neuromuscular paralysis took hold.

Jack's chest barely lifted. The ambulance's siren sounded faintly in the distance but it wasn't close enough to arrive in time. 'Starting mouth-to-mouth.' Gabe tilted Jack's chin, lowered his head and with his lips making a seal he breathed life-saving air into the child's lungs and prayed it was enough.

Elly signed off on Jack's paperwork, thankful that they'd been able to maintain his airway, avoid cardiac arrest and the risk of aspirate pneumonia. She was really pleased that together she and Gabe had achieved the best outcome for Jack, but as Midden Cove didn't have an ICU, she'd transferred him by air ambulance to Hobart. The moment the chopper had taken off and banked, Gabe had looked at his watch and said, 'El, I need to go.'

She'd recognised the look. The 'I'm a parent with responsibilities that are solely mine' look, and the ice-queen had resurfaced to try and soften the jab of her own heartache. 'Of course you need to go.'

That had been fifteen minutes ago. As she

dropped the file into the out-basket, she pictured Gabe sitting in the triplets' bedroom, playing his guitar and singing them to sleep. She could imagine Ben listening quietly, Lucy trying to use the cot as a trampoline and being told she had to lie still or there'd be no song, and Rory would have started singing anyway. Their personalities were all so different but their exuberance had snared her and she adored spending time with them.

Careful, they're not yours.

I know that, but spending time with them is easier than with Gabe. But even that bit of insight didn't stop the empty feeling around her heart intensifying.

So how do you truly feel about Gabe?

Sometimes she hated her subconscious but was it time to work out how she really felt? For sure she'd loved Gabe once, and she'd experienced a long time of hating him, but right now she didn't love him or hate him, but her body kept responding to him as if programmed by the past. If she was honest, she just wanted things to be less strained between them.

She dropped her white coat into a linen-skip,

walked out of the hospital and headed toward the car park before she realised her car was still at Bluff Point. The warm evening air tickled her bare shoulders and she decided a walk was just what she needed to blow away all the confusion and trauma of the last few hours. She'd ring the police sergeant after she'd had a meal and then catch a lift out to collect her car.

Happy with her plan, she turned into the street, breathing in the delicious aroma of the lemon-scented gums, and smiled as lorikeets zipped past low and loud, their bright blue feathers reminding her of Gabe's eyes. Her phone buzzed as a text arrived and she pulled it out of her pocket

'Need to see you. Dev.'

She sighed as threads of unease wove through her. Her fingers texted back, 'Tomorrow—E' and she promised herself she really *would* talk to him tomorrow—she owed him that after a week of brief phone calls and using work as an excuse not to see him. But she needed to be well rested and on top of things to have the hard conversation she knew she had to have with him.

She took the coast road, loving the sound of the

pounding surf, and then struck back through ti-tree grove until she intersected with the lane that ran down the side of her garden. As she reached the corner, she heard the tinkle of a bell and her silver-grey Burmese jumped up onto the front fence with a plaintive 'meow' and nuzzled his face against hers.

'What a lovely welcome home.'

'I'm glad you think so because I was starting to think you were ignoring me.'

A tremor of shock ran through her as she turned from the cat. 'Dev.'

'Eleanor.' He leaned in and kissed her cheek before his gaze swept across her tiny halter-bikini top and cut-off shorts. He opened the gate for her to pass through, his expression tinged with disapproval. 'Where have you been?'

A spurt of exasperation fizzed inside her, fol-lowed by a rush of disappointment that he didn't look at her with any hint of desire. If he had, perhaps her life wouldn't be this current fiasco. *Dream on, you know it wouldn't change a thing because it's not him you want.*

Shut up!

'I was at the rock-pools when a kid got bitten by a blue-ring octopus and I lost my favourite T-shirt to the cause. It doesn't affect my ability to practise medicine, although Gabe had to convince the father I really was a doctor.'

Dev's eyes narrowed as they stepped into the house. 'I thought you had meetings in Hobart this morning.'

'I did and then I went to do a practice rock-pool ramble so I'd be ready for next week and Gabe, his parents and children just happened to be there.' She didn't mention that the ramble had been her suggestion as a way of spending time with Gabe and the triplets, because she didn't want to hurt Dev any more than she knew she would.

He fished into her clean laundry basket and silently handed her a T-shirt. She stared at it for a moment before accepting it with a sigh of resignation, and pulled it over her head. 'Would you like a glass of wine?' She grabbed a bottle from the fridge door, needing Dutch-courage for the conversation ahead.

'No.' He folded his arms across his chest. 'I'm

here because the town is rife with rumours about you and this Gabe Lewis.'

Guilt dragged through her. 'I told you; I knew Gabe in Melbourne and we're just friends.' *Make that trying to be friends.* The lines seemed very blurred as they lurched from total strangers to a type of closeness that made her question if there might be something more between them. But whenever she did, the distance would surge back in, making her second-guess everything and leaving her more confused than ever.

She'd had a few guy friends in her adult life but none of those friendships had been anything like this. There were moments—like this afternoon when Gabe had strung Neptune's necklace around her—when she swore he was looking at her like he wanted sex right there and then, but other times his gaze was cool and distant. Perhaps it really was impossible for ex-lovers to think they could ever be friends and they both needed to accept the ex meant estranged for ever.

Dev dropped his arms and stepped in close, staring down at her, his brown eyes serious and trusting.

Don't trust me, Dev. I kissed another man without giving you a thought.

He spoke softly. 'So I have nothing to worry about?'

She couldn't meet his gaze and she stepped back in case he tried to touch her. 'Dev, I'm telling you the truth. Gabe and I are just friends.'

'I believe you, Eleanor.'

You shouldn't. She gulped in a breath. 'But we have been more than friends in the past.'

He stilled. 'But that's over now, right?'

Her heart cramped so hard she almost cried out. 'Yes. That's over. He only wants friendship.'

A light of comprehension dawned on Dev's face, casting a shadow through his eyes. 'But you want more than that?'

His words bounced around her, knocking into her like hailstones—jagged and harsh. With a rush of heart-wrenching clarity she realised that was exactly what she wanted. She wrung her hands. 'Dev, I'm sorry.'

'But he isn't offering you a future, is he?'

'No.' One syllable had never been so hard to get out.

He shook his head as if trying to sort through the information. 'He's only here on holiday, Eleanor, and then he'll leave. But we live here, we belong, and I can give you the family and the life you want.'

A tiny part of her so badly wanted to believe that because it would be the easy way out, but the once tempting thought no longer held any appeal. 'I'm sorry, Dev. I thought I wanted what you're offering, I really did, and I thought we could make it work, but there's no chemistry.'

He snorted. 'Chemistry's overrated. We have a shot at married life filled with family and being part of Midden Cove because that's what we both want. Are you prepared to throw away a chance with me for a lifetime of being alone and childless? Is that what you really want?'

Pain ricocheted through her hard and fast as his words sketched the truth like charcoal on paper. Solid, real and unavoidable—a life alone.

Once again he closed the gap between them. 'Eleanor, my offer stands and I can forgive you this lapse if you promise me you won't see him or any of his family again.'

She thought of Gabe and the triplets, of the fact that if she agreed, today would be the last time she spent any time with them. A hollow feeling opened up inside her. 'And if I can't promise you that?'

'Then my offer's null and void, and you're a fool who's throwing away what she wants most on an empty dream.'

Burning white pain crushed her as his words rained down on her. *God help her, he was right.* Dev was her last opportunity at marriage and a family, the thing she'd wanted so desperately two years ago that she'd left Gabe to chase it. Now Gabe had children but he didn't want her, and Dev was her only chance.

Make sure this guy is the one.

Dev will give you a solid life and without him you're alone.

But not even the stark truth could change her mind. *I don't love him.* 'Goodbye, Dev.'

He stared at her for a long moment, his expression stony, and then he silently turned and left. She heard the door slam and her breath whooshed out of her lungs as her body started shaking. With trembling hands, she somehow managed to open the wine bottle, poured an enormous glass and drank it down, trying hard to ignore Dev's words, which ran on constant replay in her head.

You're a fool with nothing.

Furious with him and herself, she tore off her T-shirt. 'My bikini is perfectly respectable.' She refilled the wineglass, opened an enormous packet of chips and fell onto the couch in a wave of despair. *Perhaps I am a fool.* Her cat came in through the cat-flap, jumped onto the couch, padded over to her lap and did his usual ceremonial circling until he sat down, purring. Tears threatened as she stroked him—she was going to become the crazy old lady with cats who died alone.

She drank more wine, ate chips and contemplated opening peppermint chocolate chip ice cream, but that meant getting up off the couch and disturbing Hector, and she lacked the energy to move. The heat of the cat trickled through her, the sun started to sink, the wine made her drowsy and she drifted off into an uneasy doze.

The sharp ring of her doorbell woke her with

a start and Hector jumped down with a look of haughty distain.

'Don't blame me, mate, I didn't ring the bell.' She immediately wondered who had and as she padded down the hall she caught sight of herself in the mirror. Her usual neat bob of hair looked like she'd just touched a Van de Graff generator, and black rings circled her eyes. She couldn't do anything about the circles but the hair she could control. Using her fingers, she tried to comb it into a slightly less wild state.

The bell rang again, this time for longer, as if someone was leaning on the button. It was rare for anyone to come to the house for medical care but she realised with a shock that if it was an emergency, she was going to have to ring Gabe to cover for her because she'd just drunk half a bottle of wine.

'Coming.' She hauled open the heavy oak front door and gaped. 'Gabe?'

'El.'

He stood on her veranda, and from his boat-shoe-clad feet to his the tips of his golden hair, which glinted in the fire of the setting sun, he was decadently handsome and completely out of reach to her. Heat and ice, need and want, desire and lust poured through her, leaving no space or crevice untouched.

He held up a bottle of wine. 'I raced off before we debriefed.'

Mesmerised, she stared at him, barely hearing his words, and the tiny part of her brain that hadn't leaked into a puddle of yearning thought there should be a law against him wearing royal blue. The colour made his eyes—eyes that were sweeping her from top to toe—light up with sparkle and shimmers as they morphed through every shade from azure to French navy.

His gaze roved up her legs, caressed her midriff and then lingered on her breasts, which instantly tingled and tightened, sending her nipples budding against the tiny triangles of Lycra. The rest of her body followed as tiny seeds of heat detonated, sending out more and more fire until her body was liquid heat, and her muscles melted. She swallowed a moan and gripped the door for support.

His body tensed and he raised his head to hers.

Desire and need for her shone so brightly in his eyes that this time there was no way she could mistake it for anything else. He wanted her.

No, he wants your body.

I want his. So help her, she did.

You're a fool with nothing and sex isn't going to help.

Yes, it will.

She wanted to block out how she'd completely messed up her life with bad decisions. She needed to forget that wanting everything her own way, not trusting him or giving him time had led her to this point of being childless and alone. She knew without a doubt that Gabe would go back to his life in Melbourne and that she had no part in it, but she wanted to have sex with him just one more time before she faced the empty life she'd created for herself.

She reached out her hand, folding her fingers around his open-necked shirt and pulled herself into him. She rose up on tiptoe, her lips finding his, and it was like coming home. He tasted of cinnamon, coffee and happiness, and she wrapped her arms around his neck like she'd always done, and lost herself in the wonder of his mouth.

She sensed a slight hesitation in him and deepened the kiss, revisiting his mouth in a way only a past lover could, calling him back through powerful shared memories—the times they'd lost hours to exploring each other's bodies. He groaned against her lips and reached around her, putting the wine on her hall table. Then his arms instantly circled her waist, holding her tightly against him and evaporating all space between them until their bodies moulded together as one.

Like two bolts of lightning colliding, his tongue met hers for an instant and then he plundered her mouth; going straight to the places that cranked simmering need into burning passion.

Heat spiralled inside her, filling her empty well, and need drove her onward because she wanted so much more than his mouth. Pulling his shirt free of his waistband, she ran her hands along his back, desperate to touch ripped muscle and golden skin and return to places she'd pined for since she'd left him.

His fingers buried themselves in her hair as his mouth left her lips, trailing across her cheek before his tongue started tracing the outline of her ear. Stars exploded behind her eyes, and her head tilted back both in invitation and demand, insisting that he extend his touch in a dance as old as time.

His mouth weaved its magic along her jaw and down her throat. Her breasts, heavy and throbbing, ached for the touch of his hand and as if reading her mind, his fingers slid under her halter top. When his thumb grazed her nipple, she bucked against him, and as his free hand gripped her buttock she rose up, wrapping her legs around his waist, desperate for any pressure against her quivering core.

Carrying her, he staggered backwards further into the house, and then he leaned her against the wall, his eyes burning with need. 'Elly, what are we doing?'

His voice rasped out the words that should have acted as a brake to make her really think things though, but she didn't want to listen. She cupped his face in her hands. 'Having sex.'

His chest heaved as he leaned his forehead against hers and ground out the words, 'Friends don't have sex.'

She steeled herself against the searing pain that he only wanted her to be his friend. 'So, we can be friends with benefits.'

Wide black discs obliterated the blue of his eyes. 'El, are you sure this is all you want? Friendship and casual sex?'

No, I want much more but I'll take this and make it work for me. Her throat tightened against the words. 'Sure, why not? I've been working really hard and I deserve the occasional booty call while you're here.'

He stilled. 'And the other bloke?'

She didn't want to talk about Dev or even think about him. She slid down his body, kissing him hard and fast, just the way he liked it. 'Do you want to have sex with me or not?'

'God, yes.' He returned the kiss, taking her breath with it, and then broke away, running his hand through his hair in agitation. 'We can't.'

No, don't say that. Frustration screamed in her

veins. 'We can. After all, there's nothing stopping us.'

'Common sense should be stopping us, Elly.'

The anguished expression on his face tore through her and suddenly she understood. She understood his fear and knew viscerally that his pain was her pain, but for a very different reason. 'I'm not Jenna, Gabe. I've got condoms and you can use two if you want to. I promise you, I won't get pregnant.'

But you'd like that more than anything because you love him.

Oh, dear God, she truly loved him. The realisation brought fresh waves of pain. She loved him with every part of her and he could never know.

His eyes stared into hers, grave and determined. 'Elly, we can't go back to the way we once were.'

His words rained down on her and she steeled herself against the inconvenient truth. Giving Gabe her best winning smile, she prepared to lie through her teeth as she took the first step on a road of preservation by self-delusion. 'I'm just in this for the fun.'

She led him into her bedroom and stopped just in front of the bed, a heady wave of feminine power streaking through her and burying the truth. 'And now I want to see you naked.'

His eyes sparkled. 'You're seducing me so shouldn't you be the one getting naked?'

'I prefer it this way.'

'Fine.' The word came out deep and husky as the strands of their history pulled them closer together. 'There's just one rule and that's you can look but not touch. You break it and we play by my rules.'

She laughed. 'Easy.'

One brow rose but his gaze stayed fixed on her face as he slowly unbuttoned his shirt and slipped it off his wide, tanned shoulders.

Her palms tingled as she feasted on the sight of his sculpted chest, remembering how amazing it felt to touch—toned and tough yet silky soft—then, as he dropped the shirt at her feet, her eyes drifted to his abdomen and the trail of golden hair that speared downward to the prize below. Her breath came faster.

His fingers rested on his belt. 'So how's this working for you?'

'Great.' The word sounded strangled as her body throbbed and demanded to be sated.

His laugh was wicked and, oh, so slowly he pulled the leather through the silver buckle and then slid the entire length free of the bands. His eyes bored into her so full of unmasked desire and with a need that matched her own, that it took every ounce of control not to throw her arms around his neck.

His hands settled on his waistband and he undid the button. The pants slipped to mid-hip, exposing the designer band of his boxers. His fingers eased the material millimetre by millimetre, excruciatingly slowly, and over the bulge within.

Her gaze was fixed on the bunched material and her body vibrated with anticipation as she remembered how beautiful he was—how long and hard and smooth and hot. Her blood pounded so fast she swayed, and her muscles screamed for him. Suddenly her feet were moving and her hands were on him, tugging the shorts out of the way, desperate to touch and taste and hold and caress.

Then his hands were on her, her feet were off the floor and her back abruptly slammed against the bed. His laughter rained down on her as he gently pinned her under him by straddling her on all fours.

'Hey!' She mock protested, reaching up to stroke his face.

He brushed her lips with his. 'You broke, so it's my rules now.'

'You didn't play fair.'

He grinned, his eyes glinting with anticipation. 'I played to win and now you just have to wait your turn.'

His hands brought hers above her head and she let him hold them there, her trust in him absolute. His mouth started a long, slow, burning trail from her mouth, down her jaw, and along her neck, while his hand undid her halter top. It fell away and then his mouth covered her breast and he suckled her, his tongue abrading the nipple. Streams of wonder unfurled from deep inside her, pouring through her, building on each other and tantalising her until her head thrashed against the pillow with the sheer frustration of it not being enough.

'My turn.' The words came out on a wail as her hands tugged against his grip, wanting to touch him, but he shook his head.

His mouth trailed down her belly and his hand undid the top of her shorts. She lifted her hips and for a second he used both his hands to tug the denim out of the way but then he recaptured her hands.

His eyes stared down into hers. 'You're beautiful, Elly.'

'So are you.'

He lowered his mouth and continued his delicious torture.

Her body screamed for him with ragged need. She wanted him so badly—needed him to fill her completely and stop the ache inside her—she thought she'd go mad. But then his mouth touched her most intimate place and all coherent thought vanished as her body took over, streaking away from frustration, consumed only with spiralling need that demanded complete and utter surrender. She gave in to it, letting Gabe send her flying beyond herself to a place with no mistakes.

She opened her eyes as she came back to earth. 'Thank you. You've still got it.'

He grinned. 'Oh, yeah.'

Her hands reached up and her fingers walked down his chest, across his abdomen and down, down, down until they circled what they'd ached to touch for so long.

Every part of him stilled. 'Sweetheart, be very careful or you could end up very disappointed.'

'Not possible.' She kissed him as she guided him into her; his heat merging with hers.

With her legs wrapped around him, her arms clinging to him, she rose with him, matching him stroke for stroke until their movements were one. With a cry, he shattered first, his release catching hers and propelling her up with him toward the stars, where they hovered together for an instant before parting for separate journeys down.

CHAPTER NINE

THE triplets, with buckets of water in one hand and brushes in the other, were 'painting' the old concrete path that led down to the clothes-line. Gabe smiled as he watched them and gave thanks to the sunshine for drying the job quickly so they just kept painting. He'd been smiling a lot lately.

Sex with Elly had always been amazing but this last week had been incredible. When she rang he never knew if she was calling because she needed help at the hospital or clinic, or if it was because she wanted sex, but just seeing her name on the liquid display of his phone made him hard.

When they'd been together, Elly had never been shy, but she'd never been this upfront before either. Her suggestion of friends with benefits had been a completely unexpected but welcome gift after the many nights of fitful sleep filled with dreams of her naked and totally responsive beneath him.

A ripple of unease moved through him, taking him by surprise. *Things didn't work out with that bloke.* He'd never liked the idea of her being with Dev but did their breakup have anything to do with why he and Elly were now having sex?

Nah. He reassured himself they'd both put their cards on the table; he'd told her they couldn't go back and she'd told him it was just sex and insisted on using contraception. He trusted her implicitly but it reminded him that when he got back to Melbourne he really needed to spend a day at a clinic and have a vasectomy so he never had to worry about another accidental pregnancy ever again. That decision made, he let go of a breath he hadn't realised he'd been holding and relaxed again, losing himself in the recollections of how fantastic the sex continued to be.

Despite how much she'd hurt him and he'd hurt her, despite the fact he could never make a relationship work, he still craved her body. The fact she craved his made things perfect. They'd found being friends difficult but they made fabulous sex partners. The excitement of grabbing moments when both of them were free had him constantly buzzing in anticipation, although he always found the time too short and he hated leaving her alone in her bed. But introducing Elly as a sex mate to his parents just wasn't something he was prepared to do, for all their sakes.

He wondered what Elly was doing right now. Usually she rang him but he hadn't heard from her in twenty-four hours and he had a sudden urge to hear her voice.

He pulled out his phone and called her. It rang for so long that he marshalled his thoughts, ready to leave a message on her service but then her voice came down the line.

'Hi. How's the tough life of a doctor on holidays treating you?'

Her enthusiasm for life eddied around him and he found himself grinning for no reason as an elusive calm settled over him. 'I've got the kids painting the path.'

She laughed. 'You're making them earn their keep from an early age.'

'Well, those grammar-school fees are expensive.'

He could hear other voices in the background, and then a rustling noise crackled down the line as if Elly had put her hand over the phone, but he could faintly hear her saying, 'Book an ECG and make an appointment with the cardiologist at Royal Hobart.'

Her voice then came back loud and clear. 'It's a bit frantic here at the moment, Gabe. Did you need something?'

'You.' He heard her sharp intake of breath and pictured her eyes shimmering with undisguised desire, the way they always did when he kissed her. His arms tensed, feeling empty.

She cleared her throat. 'I'm afraid that's not possible at the moment, Dr Lewis, because I have a waiting room of patients. I'll check my schedule and get back to you.'

The line went dead and he stared at the phone in disbelief. She'd hung up on him.

She's at work. The logic didn't come close to easing his general dissatisfaction that he couldn't talk with her when he wanted to.

His mother brought out a tray with icy poles for the triplets and two iced coffees. After they'd pulled the wrapping paper off the icy poles and the children were happily occupied eating and painting, his mother sat down next to him.

'I can't believe you've only got one more week of holidays.' She squeezed his arm. 'I love having the triplets here.'

'We'll be back at Easter and you're welcome in Melbourne any time.'

'I know, but it's not quite the same as here. You don't have the beach at the end of the street and we have to get into the car to go places where here we can walk.'

'Mum, you know I can't live in Midden Cove.'

'I wasn't suggesting it.'

His body tightened and he blew out a breath. 'I'm an A and E specialist and my skills belong in a city hospital, not a tiny joint like this.'

She gave him a piercing look. 'Are you trying to convince me, darling, or yourself?'

Her question irritated him and he didn't reply.

Cathleen sipped her drink. 'So how's the friendship thing going with Elly?'

He sighed and decided short answers were the only way to get through this. 'It's going well.'

'Don't confuse sex with friendship, Gabe, because the two never go together unless you're in a committed relationship.'

He stared at her, slack-jawed. His mother had never been so direct and on top of that he was stunned she knew because he thought he'd done a pretty good job of hiding his visits to Elly's place.

'You're a grown man and I stopped giving you advice a long time ago, but you of all people should know that sex is never simple.'

Memories of Jenna assailed him but were quickly overlaid by Elly—sexy, fun but in control. 'Mum, this is nothing like what happened with Jenna. Elly and I are just...'

What? Friends? Lovers? Exactly what are you? 'We're finding a way to move forward.'

Hah! That's an Oscar-worthy bit of denial.

Cathleen gave him a serene smile. 'Good.'

But the word was loaded with too much

expectation and hope, and it settled over him like a prickly vest, scratching at his decision to live his life his own way, which didn't include being part of a couple. Thankfully his father rounded the corner of the veranda and sat down with them.

'Good timing, Dad. There's something I want to give you both.' He pulled an envelope out of his pocket and handed it to his mother. 'The triplets and I want to thank you both for a great holiday.'

'Gabe, you didn't have to give us anything—we love having you here.'

'Mum, you're going to sleep for a month when we leave.'

James laughed indignantly. 'Sixty is the new fifty, son, and some days I look younger than you.'

'Sadly, Dad, that's true.'

'Oh, Gabe, thank you.' Cathleen's eyes shone as she waved tickets to the latest musical spectacular in Melbourne.

'And there's more.'

'What? Steak knives too?' James peered over Cathleen's shoulder as she opened up a letter.

'A night at the Windsor Hotel!' She rested her hand on James's knee and smiled up at him.

A shot of melancholy tinged with green twisted through Gabe. His parents had a close and loving relationship built on trust, the type of relationship that had always eluded him. Even Elly—the woman he'd once thought might be the one— hadn't trusted him enough to stay.

His mother suddenly frowned. 'But the date on this says Wednesday. That's before you leave.'

He nodded. 'I know. Ideally this present should be in two weeks' time, but live theatre waits for no man and the show closes next week, so it's now or never. Besides, it's only twenty-four hours and you'll be back for our last three days.'

'What about help at the crunch times with the triplets?' His mother had the look of someone about to say, 'Thanks but, no, thanks.'

He moved to reassure her. 'It'll be good practice for me because I won't have you guys to fall back on when I'm back in Melbourne.'

'You have the nannies there so you should get

someone to help out.' James stood up as Rory ran over and he swung his grandson up into his arms. 'What about Elly? She was great with the triplets at the rock pools but they haven't seen her since and Lucy keeps picking up her bucket and saying "Lee".'

Gabe experienced the familiar zip of irritation that burned whenever he thought his parents were pushing him into a relationship, and he expected his mother to chime in but she was unusually silent. The feeling faded when he noticed his father's expression was free of any agenda other than making sure he had help with the triplets.

A quiet realisation moved through him confirming that his father was right on both fronts. On the outings Elly had come along to, she'd been great with the kids, which made sense because, unlike him, she'd always had an easy affinity with children, but for some reason she hadn't seen his gang in a week.

You started having sex, remember.

He couldn't quite work out why that meant Elly hadn't spent time with the kids but, like today, she'd been working pretty hard. Hell, he'd hardly seen her except in bed, and she'd just hung up on him because of work.

Saturday. He smiled as a plan unfurled, his parents' trip to Melbourne creating a perfect situation. He and Elly could spend the whole day together and then all of the night.

'Now, *that* was worth waiting for.'

'I'd have to agree.' Elly smiled as Gabe's arms tightened around her. They lay snuggled together in her bed but it was late because she'd had a long day at the practice and there'd been no opportunity to get away any earlier to meet Gabe.

She moved to get comfortable and a sharp pain made her gasp.

'You OK?'

She blew out a breath and the pain faded. She was used to ovulation pain each month but that had happened a week ago and this was different. 'Fine. I think I must have pulled a muscle today when I was lifting some heavy boxes. Why is it that the *one* thing you need from newly delivered supplies is always at the bottom?'

'Murphy's law, but you need to be careful you

don't give yourself a hernia.' His breath tickled her ear. 'You know you could have asked me to come in today and help.'

'Although it was a full day, nothing counted as an emergency, and you're on holidays, remember.'

'I am, but being with you is a fun part of my holiday.'

Holiday sex. As a shaft of emotional pain hit her, she wrapped her arms over his, knowing that at some point within the next half-hour he'd kiss her, roll away, pull on his clothes and walk out the door back to his real life. The one she played no part in, and the reason lay at her own feet. Up until two weeks ago she'd always blamed Gabe for breaking her heart but the stark truth was she'd broken her own heart two years ago when she hadn't been prepared to give him time or trust him enough to change his mind about children.

She bit her lip against the old pain that caught her when she thought about his gorgeous triplets. She'd deliberately avoided spending more time with them in the last week because letting go of Gabe would be hard enough.

You could ask him to stay.

He stroked her hair. 'I booked tickets home on the *Spirit* today.'

Ouch. Now, that's real life.

Offer to go to Melbourne with him. The tempting thought terrified her. *No. He told me in no uncertain terms that we can't go back.*

Still, what do you have to lose if you ask him?

Pride, self-respect, everything!

Coward.

She traced the outline of his hand. 'So, you're back to the old routine?'

'Yep. Bella and Lauren start work the day after we get home and I'm back to work too.'

'Is it lonely, being a single parent?'

'I'm too busy to be lonely, Elly.' A warning note sounded in his voice.

She didn't believe him. 'Don't you miss having someone to talk to about your day, sharing what the kids did, stuff like that?'

'No one misses what they've never had.'

She heard his long sigh and felt the exhaled breath like a whip against her skin, and she ached for him. For herself. He'd never experienced a parenting partnership with someone who loved him and he had no plans to try.

He pressed a kiss onto her shoulder. 'Look, I know as my *friend* you're concerned about me but you don't have to be. I have colleagues at work to debrief with, and I have the nannies to talk to about the kids. Before you go joining in with my parents' plot to match me up with someone, the kids have plenty of women in their lives so they're not missing out either. We're fine on our own, Elly. Absolutely fine.'

And there's your answer loud and clear.

She closed her eyes, swallowed her shudder of regret and changed the subject. 'Did I tell you? Just after I wave you goodbye, my sister's bringing her twin daughters down for a beach holiday.'

'You have twin nieces?'

The surprise in his voice vibrated through her, immediately chased by her own sorrow that they could be so in tune sexually yet so far apart in other ways. 'I do.'

'IVF twins?' His voice sounded strained.

She shook her head. 'No, Suzy kept the family tradition of twins going. Every generation of my family going back eighty years has at least one set of twins. The girls are a bit younger than the triplets, which I guess is why you didn't know about them. I don't get to see much of them so I'm really looking forward to their visit.'

But talking children just amplified her own barren state and made her feel wretched so she switched topics. 'So do you have any plans for your last few days?'

'I want us to go on a farewell picnic.'

She thought of the picnics they'd gone on with the triplets and wondered if she could get through another one without her heart taking a hammering. 'That sounds lovely. Anything else?'

He ran his tongue around her ear and she immediately banished the seeds of the idea that she should ask him to stay, seeds that not only sprouted deep down inside her but were now clinging vines that threatened to choke her. She knew she should fight for him and tell him how she really felt, but she also knew she'd lost that battle when she'd walked out on him two years ago.

She loved him but he was leaving soon and she was banking memories for the dark years ahead. As he extended his kiss, she rolled in his arms and melted into him, doing the only thing she could—she kissed him back.

Gabe had waved goodbye to his parents, dressed the triplets, ordered the picnic lunch and packed snack food for the kids. He had the beach shelter, kites and every conceivable beach toy that the triplets might want stowed in the car. Everything and everyone was ready to go. All he needed was Elly.

He glanced at his watch. She'd said she'd arrive at ten and it was now a quarter past. Lucy and Rory were playing with the wooden train, although Rory kept looking up to check Gabe was close by and Ben had been very clingy since his grandparents had left. As a result, Gabe had done most of the packing with Ben in his arms. 'Hey, mate, where's Elly?'

Ben didn't even raise his head from Gabe's shoulder to look around.

'Lee. Where's Lee?' Lucy ran over from the trains.

Ben loved to swing on the front gate so perhaps if they went outside he'd get over his sads about his Nana and Pa-pa leaving. 'Let's go out into the garden and see if we can see her car.'

Lucy ran to the front door and Gabe followed, calling Rory at the same time. They spilled into the spacious and rambling garden, and Lucy clambered up onto the fence into her favourite position but Ben refused to budge out of Gabe's arms and even Rory had to be coaxed up onto the gate. They counted two dogs, waved to the Gilberts, who walked past and had a chat, and they even saw a wallaby hop by, but there was no sign of Elly.

Just as Gabe shifted Ben from one arm to the other so he could pull his phone out of his pocket, Lucy squealed. 'Lee, Lee!'

Gabe grinned, realising he was almost as excited as his daughter. Anticipation whizzed through him and he had the day planned down to the last detail—a day at the beach to exhaust the triplets, early bedtime for them and then the evening stretched ahead just for Elly and him. He had the champagne in the fridge, the prawns on ice and all he had to do was slice some mangoes and avocado, toss the rocket through the dressing, arrange it all on a plate, and that was dinner sorted. He'd bought her favourite chocolate for dessert, put fresh sheets on his bed and he had no qualms at all about handling the rest of the evening.

'Hey, guys.' Elly stepped through the gate as Lucy and Rory threw themselves at her knees. She seemed to sway back slightly before squatting down so she was at the same level as the children. 'Wow, this is a huge welcome.'

'Beach go now!' Rory pulled on her hand.

'Lee, up me.' Lucy held out her arms.

Elly laughed and swung Lucy up into her arms and tousled Rory's hair.

'You're popular.' Gabe leaned in, planning on greeting her with a friendly kiss on the cheek, but her ocean-fresh scent wove through him and his lips lingered.

Elly stepped back first. 'Sorry I'm late but I had three sick kids at the practice and I had to make a house call for one of my chemo patients.'

Her gaze skated across Gabe and he caught a fleeting glance of heat which instantly vanished as her attention centred on Ben, who was still cuddled in close to Gabe's shoulder.

'Hey, little guy, you don't look so great.' Her hand brushed his forehead. 'Ah, Gabe, Ben's very pale and I think he's got a fever.'

Please, not today. He'd wanted today to be perfect because it was going to be the last full day he and Elly would probably spend together. Sadly, a rising temperature would certainly make sense of Ben's unusually clingy behaviour. He put his lips on Ben's forehead. Hot. 'Oh, mate, I'm sorry. I thought you were just quiet because you were missing Nana and Pa-pa.'

'I prescribe paracetamol, fluids, staying at home and lots of cuddles.' Elly intercepted Lucy's hand, which was heading straight to her dangly earrings.

'Beach.' Lucy pointed down the road.

Elly seemed to take in a deep breath before she

spoke. 'Do you want me to take Rory and Lucy to the beach while you stay home with Ben?'

No! Disappointment completely out of proportion to the situation rammed him hard. Today was supposed to be all about spending time with Elly. Silently, he tried to sort through the mess and come up with the best plan.

Best for whom?

'Of course I completely understand if you're uncomfortable with that idea.'

A flash of pain flared in her eyes as she spoke, hitting him square in the solar plexus. 'God, no, of course I'm not uncomfortable with that. I trust you completely with the children.'

'Daddy.'

He looked down at Rory, whose cheeks were bright with two red spots on them and a sinking feeling rolled through Gabe's gut.

Elly followed his gaze. 'There's a twenty-four-hour virus going around.'

Rory promptly vomited on her feet.

Gabe sighed, defeat nipping at his heels. He

knew from experience that Lucy would probably
be sick within the hour. 'I think the picnic just
got cancelled.'

CHAPTER TEN

APART from the fact Elly was in Gabe's parents' home, the last nine hours had mimicked being on duty in a children's ward, except in a hospital her patients rarely put their arms around her neck or snuggled into her, just wanting to be held. The day had been a blur of damp towels, medicine cups, electrolyte solution, chicken soup, DVDs, tears, nappies and cuddles.

'I think today is what us experts in the trenches call a baptism by fire.' Gabe washed a very subdued Rory, who sat passively in the bath, a sure sign he was unwell.

She laughed. 'Baptism by vomit would be more accurate.'

He winced. 'True. Sorry about your sandals.'

She shrugged, not really caring about them at all. 'It's the perfect excuse for me to go shopping for a new pair.'

He gave a wan smile. 'I think you better bill us for today because I invited you for a picnic and you ended up working with three sick kids.'

And just like that his words inserted distance between them—the ever-present distance that reminded her she wasn't really part of his or the children's lives. She hated that her heart tore a little more because she'd been foolish enough to think that after all they'd shared today, perhaps they might have overcome it. Not wanting him to recognise her feelings, she teased, 'It's not a problem. After all, what else does a doctor want to do on her day off?'

His eyes flickered with longing. 'I had other plans, believe me.'

The familiar response—her body tightening with tingling rafts of need—shot through her. 'They'd need to be G-rated in front of the children.'

He grinned at her, all boyish charm and simmering sexuality. 'I'm hoping they'll *eventually* go to sleep tonight.'

She laughed and leaned into the bath to pick up Ben. A sharp, griping pain made her stall, and she slowly blew out a breath, feeling the pain pass as quickly as it had come. It was the same pain that had caught her in bed the other night when she'd rolled over quickly so it was probably ligament pain. She made a mental note not to make any jerky movements and next time there were heavy boxes at work, she wasn't going to move them without a trolley.

They slipped into an unspoken routine, with Elly drying each triplet and then Gabe dressing them in their pyjamas. Usually the children's exuberance made the process a challenge of drying and dressing on the run, but tonight they lacked the energy and were almost docile with occasional spurts of viral crankiness.

'Nigh' nigh'.' Ben put his arms around Gabe's neck as his thumb crept toward his mouth.

'Sing.' Rory crawled into Gabe's lap.

Lucy tugged at Elly's shorts. 'Up me.'

Elly wanted to scoop her up into her arms but Gabe leaned back and swooped her into his lap.

'Come on honey-pie, bedtime.' He stood up, carrying both a now sobbing little girl as well as

Ben. With Rory clutching at his leg, he walked out of the bathroom without looking back.

We're fine on our own. Absolutely fine.

Desperate to keep busy, Elly set about tidying the bathroom, telling herself over and over that the triplets were not hers, that Gabe had his own routine, and it was crazy to feel shut out. However, no amount of rational logic worked and she wanted to join in with the wailing too. It was as if she was being punished over and over for her ill-judged mistake in the past.

As the last of the gurgling water drained out of the bath and silence descended in the bathroom, Elly expected to hear the soothing, settling sounds of Gabe singing and the hush of children going to sleep drifting down the corridor. Instead, she heard the screeching wail of three distraught children who were feeling lousy and this was their only way of letting the world know.

'Elly.' Gabe's rich, deep voice, filled with defeated desperation, bounced off the walls.

She almost ran down the corridor and into the triplets' room. Three sobbing, red-faced children complete with runny noses greeted her, and Gabe didn't look much better. She immediately picked up Lucy, who was closest, and hugged her tight before wiping her face. 'Shh, it's really not all that bad.'

'Can you promise me that?' Gabe's fatigue surrounded him as he picked up the boys with a sigh. 'Thanks for being here.'

Of course I'm here. I want to be part of this. But her lips refused to form those words, which would only open her up to more rejection. 'I'm happy to help.'

Gabe patted the boys and pointed to his guitar. 'Daddy's going to sing to you, OK?'

But Ben refused to be put in his cot so Elly sat down on a chair with both Lucy and Ben on her lap.

After some persuasion, Rory finally lay down and Gabe picked up his guitar. His tanned fingers expertly formed the chords and he started to sing, his voice harmonising with the sound created by plectrum and strings. Elly listened to the words he'd written specifically for his trio and she had to hide her face against Lucy's curls as his love for them rolled out in the calming tune. He'd once told her he loved her but had it ever been that much?

You didn't stay to find out.

Ten chords in, Rory stood up screaming, reaching his arms out toward his siblings.

'I give up.' With a clashing strum of immense frustration, Gabe leaned the guitar up against the wall and picked up Rory.

Lucy and Ben snuggled into Elly's shoulder, illness making them crave human touch, and Elly totally understood. On the few occasions she'd got sick as an adult, the one thing she'd always pined for had been to be a little girl again. She'd dream of the times when her mother had made her chicken soup and read her stories.

She looked over at Gabe, who was clearly coming to the end of his tether. 'What about stories on the couch? They might settle and nod off.'

He looked like he wanted to hug her. 'Good idea, only not the couch because if they fall asleep there we'll have to move them and they'll wake up.'

'Where, then?'

He stared at her for a moment and then sighed. 'My bed.'

The two words came out on a long, woeful moan and she started to laugh.

His eyes flashed with indignation. 'What on earth can you find funny about this mess?'

She started to shake as the laughter took over. 'Embrace the irony, Gabe. It's the only time in living memory that you've invited me into bed with a look of utter despair.'

His stony look slowly faded and a faint smile played around his wide and generous mouth. 'Yeah, well, I put clean sheets on for you, not the triplets.' He started walking toward his room.

Elly followed with Ben and Lucy. 'I'm sure they'll appreciate it.'

'Yeah, right.' He gave a grunt of laughter. 'I mean, how could I have possibly forgotten that all toddlers appreciate Egyptian cotton sheets?'

Gabe had read one story, and then Elly had taken over and was reading her second. He lay back against a stack of pillows, letting her musical voice wash over him like soothing balm. Ben, now asleep, lay on his chest, Lucy lay on Elly's, and Rory snuggled between Elly and him, his eyes heavy but still not quite closed.

It had been a hell of a day and at times had reminded him of the dark, dark days when the triplets had just come home from hospital and Jenna had fallen apart. Every waking moment had been consumed by trying to meet their needs as his own had been subjugated to theirs, and the pressure of being responsible for everyone bore down so hard it had threatened to push him under.

Except today you laughed. Elly made you laugh.

He realised with a shock that was true. They'd juggled sick and grumpy children all day, but even when he'd been knee-deep in body fluids and sick kids, she'd made him laugh and smile. When the triplets had thrown up at virtually the same moment all over themselves, Elly had just thrown him a deadpan look and said, 'You brought that on yourself by putting them in clean clothes.'

She'd been amazing throughout it all, and

although a couple of times he'd almost lost it, she'd always lifted him up with a funny line or a reassuring touch that said she was finding it tough too. Right now, though, she looked as exhausted as he felt, but her radiance shone out despite mussed hair, no make-up and crumpled clothes.

Rory started to snore gently but Elly continued reading another page before she lowered her voice and slowed her delivery until she stopped. Her eyes shone with a well-earned victory. 'Dare I say I think we did it?'

He reached out his hand, his fingers entwining with hers. '*You* did it. You alone relaxed the Lewis clan into a soporific stupor.'

A smile danced across her high cheek-bones and she squeezed his hand. 'It's what I do.'

'Thank you.' He wanted to lean in and kiss her but he didn't risk moving and waking anyone up this early into sleep, so he lifted her hand to his mouth and pressed it against his lips. 'You do realise we're stuck here for about half an hour until they're really asleep.'

She smiled serenely. 'There are a lot worse places to be.'

'Maybe you're right.' He thought about the many places he'd laid his head over the years and couldn't remember feeling this peaceful since— *Never.* Surely that wasn't possible?

You got close with Elly before the split. But even back then he couldn't remember this sort of contentment.

She looked straight at him. 'I *am* right. War zones don't come with such soft and silky sheets.'

'Five-star hotels have the sheets but not the human heaters.' He patted Ben's back.

She chuckled. 'They do give out an amazing amount of heat.'

'Some nights they all end up in bed with me and there have been times when I've sneaked off to their room when the kicking got too much.' He grinned. 'Rory's the worst but Lucy gives him a run for his money.'

'She's going to organise her brothers.'

'And me. I can already see the writing on the

wall.' He watched mesmerised as Elly stroked Lucy's curls with her free hand.

Is it lonely, being a single parent?

For some reason, Elly's question from the other night beamed into his brain and a streak of guilt shot through him. He tried to picture lying on the bed with the triplets and Jenna, but the image wouldn't come.

You and Jenna didn't ever parent together.

But the glib words didn't ease a thing because he knew deep in his heart that even if Jenna hadn't been sick they'd have struggled to stay together to parent. God, it had been one enormous mess and the triplets and Jenna the biggest losers.

'Who was born first?' Keen interest shone in Elly's eyes.

'Lucy. She came out wide-eyed and looking around, followed by Rory. They didn't spend long in their isolettes but it was Ben who caused me the most heartache. He was smaller than the others, he spent time on the open cot and the first two weeks were a huge struggle for him.'

'I can't imagine what that sort of fear would be like.' She hooked his gaze. 'That day we evacuated Millie, you were thinking of Ben then, weren't you?'

'I was. There's nothing worse than watching your kid and knowing you can't step forward and fight the battle for them. Ben's slightly behind the others but by two he should have caught up completely.'

'He's done really well, then.' She dropped his hand and stroked Ben's back. 'I've noticed he sits back and checks out the lie of the land while the other two charge ahead. You wait; I bet he'll be your quiet achiever.'

Her words echoed his own thoughts exactly and a buzz of something warm and wonderful, something he couldn't quite name, rolled through him. He picked up her hand again. 'Do you want to know what their first words were after the usual *dada*?'

'Tell me.'

'Rory said, "Ball".'

'That makes sense; he's always got a ball in his hand. I bet Lucy said a command word, like "More" or "Mine".'

He laughed at her accuracy. 'It was "Up" and

Ben said "Byebye" at ten months and didn't say it again until the other day.'

Like a plug being pulled, he found himself talking about the triplets, telling her about their milestones and regaling her with funny stories and their idiosyncrasies until he suddenly stopped, realising he'd been talking for twenty minutes. 'Sorry, I'm sounding like the world's most boring father.'

She shook her head and slid her hand over his. 'No, you're sounding like the proud father you are. You should do it more often.' She suddenly looked self-conscious. 'I mean, you probably do, right, talk about them to your colleagues, on the phone to your parents and with the nannies.'

'Yeah, I do.' *But it doesn't feel anything like this.*

Don't you miss having someone to talk to about your day? When Elly had asked him that question, he'd hotly contested it, but now his answer seemed as empty as the reality.

The triplets slept on, relaxed and cocooned in the vibes that spun through him, tugging at every part of him, demanding that it not end. Was this connectedness, this feeling of contentment, this sense of togetherness, and the feeling of 'I'm here for you' that flowed so strongly between them, was this what it might have been like if they'd stayed together and had a child?

All those feelings—they're called love.

A shot of tension ricocheted through him. *No, it's not love.* He'd loved Elly once before and it had *never* felt quite like this. He was certain it wasn't love. It didn't come with a euphoric high or gut-wrenching pain, but it felt so much stronger than friendship.

Tendrils of an idea sprouted and spread through him rapidly like the voracious growth of jungle vines.

Life with Elly. He could picture himself coming home to Elly and the triplets. Imagine them as a team of five. She'd always wanted children and he had three to give her.

Jenna didn't have this chance.

His shame immediately tried to surface, only to be howled down by blinding perception.

Honour Jenna through the children.

Like a missing piece of a puzzle, everything

slotted into place with a thud. This was it. This was exactly what that meant. He'd been running from the idea of a relationship to protect himself and the children, but he could see now that they needed a mother who'd love them as her own. Elly was doing that already and the thought of going back to Melbourne without her held no appeal at all.

The vines of these nameless feelings tugged at his heart but without causing any pain, hurt or exhilaration. They fitted somewhere between friendship and love, and at that moment he knew he didn't ever want to let them go. Elly would make their family complete—two parents, three kids and maybe a dog. Perfection.

'Marry *us.*'

If Elly hadn't been lying down she would have fallen over. Her blood instantly swooped to her feet, leaving a roaring in her ears as her brain tried to work out if she'd really heard those two words. Of all the questions she might have anticipated from Gabe, a marriage proposal wasn't one of them. 'Excuse me?'

His hand tightened around hers as he gazed into her eyes. 'Come back to Melbourne with us and make our family complete.'

She stared at him as happiness swirled through her like water charging through a gorge, flooding her with sheer and utter bliss. Lying here with Gabe and the children had been the most wonderful experience of her life and his question, although completely unexpected, was the completion of a dream come true.

Why now?

But she didn't care why he'd chosen right this minute to propose, a time when they were covered in children and she couldn't throw herself into his arms, but she knew she'd just been given exactly what she wanted. 'Yes. Oh, very much, yes.'

His hand reached over Rory and stroked her cheek. 'Imagine I'm kissing you with joy.'

She caught his hand with her free one, kissing his fingers and tracing them with her tongue.

He shuddered, his eyes dark with longing. 'I think it's time we tried to put these kids in their cots so we can really celebrate. I'll take Ben first and then come back for Rory.'

She nodded, shaking with happiness as she watched him carry Ben from the room. Rory stirred and she patted his back, and he rolled over and slept on. Gazing at the children, she finally let go of the barriers she'd unsuccessfully tried to hold in place, letting her heart open completely to them, knowing they were truly hers.

Gabe padded back, sliding his arms under Rory and silently carried him out of the room. Elly swung her feet to the floor and followed. She lowered Lucy slowly into her cot, keeping her close to her for as long as possible and quickly tucking the light summer quilt over her to try and avoid a rush of wakening, cold air. Then she quietly backed out of the room.

Gabe carefully closed the door with the softest click and with his finger to his lips he caught her around the waist and kissed her until she was boneless with need and delirious with happiness. In a fumble of feet and hands, they stumbled back into his room, discarding clothes as they went, and the moment he closed the door, he pulled her onto the bed covering her body with his.

His mouth never left hers, his tongue branding her as his own, taking her breath and exchanging it with his. The intensity stunned her and she rose up toward him, urging him on, and the moment he entered her she knew that this time she was home. Fast, hot and frenzied, they quickly rose together toward the stars and spilled over into ecstasy, bonded together as one.

'So finally a real celebration.'

Gabe's smile cascaded over Elly as she sat adjacent to him at a small, linen-covered restaurant table, loving it that he kept leaning in to kiss her. It totally made up for the fact she'd felt slightly under-par all day, as if she was fighting a virus. She raised her glass of champagne to his and smiled. 'I thought Saturday night was a pretty good celebration.'

'Oh, yeah.' He grinned at her, his eyes sparkling dangerously with undisputed desire. 'That goes without saying, but this dinner is just us because the moment we tell my parents, that's going public and the craziness starts, with everyone weighing in with congratulations and opinions.'

He traced the length of her ring-finger on her left hand. 'By the way, I know you like sapphires, rubies and diamonds so I've rung a jeweller in Melbourne to sketch some designs but if you have anything in mind, you can talk to him tomorrow.'

'I haven't given rings much thought.' Elly was still deliciously floating on air with occasional moments of total incredulity, and her brain was in a permanent state of bliss.

'Now's the time, then.' He captured her entire hand in his. 'There's a heap of things to organise, including when you leave Midden Cove.'

The thought of cutting her ties with the town saddened her. 'I guess I have to leave because there isn't a job here for you unless you've considered working at the Royal?'

His eyes widened in surprise and his reply was slow to come. 'What about we buy a shack down here for holidays and that way you can get your Midden Cove fix and the triplets get their grandparent fix?'

'That sounds like a wonderful idea.'

'Great. Now, back to when you think you can leave the Cove.'

She thought of Jeff, who wasn't even halfway through his trip. 'I need to give my partner notice and the earliest would be two months but probably more likely to be three.'

'Three months.' Gabe frowned. 'I really want you in Melbourne with us as soon as possible.'

The floating feeling got slightly bumped by reality. 'I want that too but I can't leave until there's a doctor here, Gabe, you know that.'

'Hmm. What if we could get a locum in earlier?'

'If Jeff was OK with that, and I can't see why he'd object, then it might just work. I'll email him tonight.'

'I'll draft an ad for you so it's ready to go and I'll put the word out to see if anyone at Melbourne Central fancies a change down here.'

He leaned in and kissed her again. 'One problem partially solved. Now, for the wedding. March in Melbourne is a great time for a wedding.'

This time reality slammed into floaty and Elly tumbled back to earth. 'But that's only weeks away. My mother will have a fit.'

His thumb stilled its wondrous caresses on the back of her hand. 'It doesn't have to be a big wedding, does it? I thought we could get married at the registry office and go for lunch at Florenzzi's afterwards.'

'Oh.' A jab of disappointment caught her by surprise and a tiny ripple of concern washed against her happiness. This was to be her first and only wedding and although she understood he'd been married before, that hadn't been the love match she shared with him. She put down her glass and held both his hands. 'It doesn't have to be a huge wedding but I want to walk down the aisle on my father's arm and stand proudly next to you, in front of our family and friends.'

He kissed her affectionately on the nose. 'Just promise me no horse and carriage and no meringue wedding dress, and I'm there.'

'You're on.' She hugged a smile to herself. In

the past they'd have argued, each stubbornly holding their ground, unable to compromise, but they'd just negotiated a middle ground with spectacular ease.

The waiter brought a taster plate of entrées, which looked like a work of art with a tiny goat's cheese and pumpkin tart, a miniature Vietnamese rice paper roll and a variety of seafood from octopus to tiger prawns, but Elly's normally ravenous appetite had vanished. She put it down to the constant fizz of excitement that had filled her from the moment Gabe had proposed and by default had given her what she wanted most in the world. *Almost.*

Gabe swallowed his morsel of Tasmanian trout marinated in Campari and chervil. 'So we've covered your job here and the wedding. I guess we should talk about our home.'

Our home. The sweet feeling of belonging rushed in so fast she felt hot and dizzy, and she needed to rest her head on his shoulder for a moment before she could speak. 'How would you feel if I didn't work full time? I'd really like to work a couple of sessions a week in a family practice and spend the rest of the week at home with the triplets.'

He leaned in close, his forehead touching hers and his eyes ablaze with delight. 'I'd hoped you'd want to do that.' He tucked her hair behind her ear. 'We can work out the nannies' rosters around your job and mine, and sometimes or at all times, you might want some help on your at-home days. I know I do.'

She kissed him, loving him so much she thought she'd explode from the joy. 'And I was thinking, when the triplets are two we could start trying for a baby brother or sister for them.'

He tensed and lifted his head away from hers, slowly straightening up in his chair. 'I think that's a bit soon, El.'

His answer surprised her. 'Really? Why?'

A muscle twitched in his jaw. 'Because four kids under three would be beyond stressful.'

Old feelings of anger, sadness and disappointment started to rise slowly from deep inside her. *You want everything your own way.* Gabe had levelled that criticism at her and he'd been right. Forcing herself to take a deep breath, she focused on keeping calm and relaxed because if she'd learned anything, it was that her reactions had played a major role in their break-up last time. Back then she'd lost everything and there was no way was she risking losing it again, and more. They'd just compromised on work and the wedding with a minimum of fuss and they could compromise on this.

She reached for his hand again. 'I guess you're right, it would be pretty full on. What about we start trying when they're at kinder? Then when the baby arrives the triplets will be at school.'

'That's just when our life will be getting easier, El.' His gaze bored into hers, his blue eyes filled with unusually serious strands of colour. 'You know what they're like now, totally full on and then some, but once they're at school you and I will have the time to do things as a couple as well as a family.'

This time you have to trust him. Elly struggled to keep her faith as the loud ticking of her biological clock almost deafened her. 'OK, so when do you think is a good time to start?'

He shrugged, his shoulders rising in a gesture

of vacillation but settling into rolled-back res-
oluteness. 'We already have three gorgeous
children.'

She leaned even closer. 'I know and I love them
with all of me, but I want to have a baby and give
them the joy of having a younger sibling.'

A chilly tension touched his cheeks. 'We're a
family the way we are.'

Her mouth dried and her heart hit her ribcage
with a sickening thud. 'Are you saying you don't
want to have another child? A child with me?'

He kissed her gently on the forehead. 'Elly,
with your age and your family history of twins
in every generation, we could go from three to
five in a heartbeat.'

She tried to stave off the rising panic that this
was a repeat performance of their stand-off two
years ago. She somehow forced her tight-with-
tension cheek muscles up into a smile. 'So we'd
have a tennis team.'

His mouth flattened. 'It isn't funny, El. My three
alone will stretch us.' He ran his hand through
his hair. 'Hell, after the other night you know the
workload with the triplets—and what about us?

We count, Elly. I want a long and happy marriage like my parents' and more children would only stress us.'

'No, it won't and, besides, it's not a given that I would have twins, just a chance.' The fight for her yet-to-be conceived child buzzed through her with the protection of a lioness for her cub. 'We're a team, Gabe, and we have help from the nannies, your parents and my parents. We can do this—a baby will strengthen us.'

She cupped his face with her hands. 'I love the triplets, that's not in any doubt at all, but I want to experience the wonder of motherhood, not only from fifteen months but from the very beginning.' Her hand fisted against her chest. 'I want to feel your child growing inside me.'

She hauled in another breath and stared deep into his eyes, seeing his apprehension and un-derstanding it in part. 'You know I want a child, you've known it for almost as long as I have. Last time you once accused me of not listening to you and not trusting you enough. I know right now the thought of more children and the chance of twins is overwhelming for you, but you're a fabulous father and you're going to relax into this over time and change your mind.'

He leaned back slightly. 'What we have is special, El, but it will sink under the onslaught of five or more children and slowly shrivel and die. We can't risk losing us.'

His fear rolled into her and she moved to reassure and soothe. 'Like I told you two weeks ago, I'm not Jenna, Gabe. I'm not going to lie to you or tamper with contraception. I'm not going to have a baby without your agreement and we'll use contraception until you're ready.'

His eyes flickered with shadows and a sad smile attempted to tug at his lips. 'That's good to know, but I really think the best thing is if I have a vasectomy.'

No! Her breath turned to solid ice in her chest, the burning cold numbing her from tip to toe. Dear God, it really was happening all over again, only this time it was ten times worse because she loved him even more and she loved his children.

This is so not fair! Every part of her wanted to storm out at the unjustness of the situation.

Be mature. Stay. Make it work.

She'd never done anything so hard in her life and she could hardly frame the words but she forced them across rigid lips. 'A vasectomy's virtually irreversible and it will just cause massive problems for us when you change your mind.'

'I won't change my mind, Elly. I made this decision before Jenna died and the only reason I haven't acted on it was lack of time and necessity. But now is the time and it's more important than ever.' He touched her arm. 'I'm doing it for us.'

She wanted to scream, yell, shout and cry but she dug deep and hauled on every cell of reasoning, trying to follow his line of thinking. 'For us? How do you see that?'

Sincerity lined his face, rooted in deep belief. 'A vasectomy means no accidents and it will protect us as a couple.'

Gabe's words hammered her, making no sense. She tried to slow down her racing thoughts, tried to work out what was really going on. Did it have anything to do with Jenna?

He'd told her he didn't want another relationship

and then he'd proposed to her, so surely that meant he was completely over his first marriage?

Think. He knew she wanted children because they'd broken up over this very issue two years ago so why would he even propose marriage to her if he didn't want them to have a child together?

Marry us.

Us. Him and the children.

She desperately tried to remember what else he'd said when he'd proposed. *Imagine I'm kissing you with joy.* Joy.

Not love.

The truth ripped through her with unspeakable pain and silver spots floated before her eyes. He didn't love her. She knew he admired her and desired her, but he didn't love her. He'd might have loved her once but not any more.

He loves the triplets.

Come back to Melbourne with us and make our family complete.

And there it was, the reason he'd proposed. She wanted to sob on the cruel irony. She'd challenged him on why he was locking women out of his life and how the triplets needed a mother and that was why he'd changed his mind—he wanted her as the mother for his children.

This time she didn't misunderstand him. This time she was not at fault. She'd offered compromise and he'd refused. He had his children and he didn't want any more. If he loved her he'd want a child with her and understand why she needed their baby in her life.

She stifled a cry as hot and cold chills raced through her and her heart bled until the only thing left behind was a dry and arid wasteland. Gabe was no different from Dev. He wanted her in his life for his own reasons and her wants and needs didn't count.

'Elly, the triplets are as much yours as mine.' Gabe broke the long silence, hating the way Elly's face had paled, apart from two bright spots of colour burning on her cheeks and making her look feverish. He'd thought the triplets would be enough for her because the idea of more children had him running scared, given what he'd been through with Jenna. No way was he risking losing this special bond he had with Elly by the arrival of more children.

He had to make her understand. 'You're their mother in every sense of the word but I can have formal papers drawn up so you can legally adopt them if that makes you feel better.'

She shook her head, her green eyes grim. 'I love the triplets and formalising my role isn't the problem. The idea of the vasectomy is the problem.'

He sighed. 'I'm being practical, El. We have three kids already and can you really imagine us with another set of twins?'

She pressed her lips together. 'Up until two minutes ago I absolutely could, but now I can't.'

Relief filled him that they'd reached agreement. He brought her hand to his mouth and kissed it. 'It's the right decision and it will protect us so we last long into the future.'

She tugged her hand away, her neck and jaw rigid. 'No, Gabe, it will destroy us.'

A jet of fear tore through him as memories of the past rose up like spectres. 'I'm giving you three children, Elly. *Three.* An instant family.

Surely that's more than enough to fill the nurturing hole inside you.'

'You really believe that, don't you?' She sounded inexplicably sad.

'I do.' He dropped his head close, breathing in her scent and her vitality, and stroked her cheek. 'We're great together and we'll make wonderful parents for the three we've got and still have time for a life, not to mention an amazing sex life.'

She jerked in her chair as if she'd been shocked. 'You've got it all figured out, haven't you? I mean, perish the thought we went a week without sex.'

'It would be a lot longer than a week.' The moment the muttered words came out he wanted to grab them back. 'I'm sorry, sweetheart, of course it isn't just about the sex. It's about how hard it is for a relationship to survive the first year with a baby or, in our case, probably twins. You think it will be fine but I know the challenges because I've lived through them. Believe me, I'm only thinking of us when I say not having more children is the best thing for our future.'

She drained her glass of champagne in one

gulp and hit him with a look that seared. 'You once accused me of not listening to you but now you're not listening to me. How many times do I need to tell you I'm not Jenna?'

Frustration poured through him. 'I know you're not Jenna but you know the stats for postnatal depression after giving birth? I can't live through all that again, Elly. I can't risk losing you.'

Her eyes glinted like steel. 'Do you love me, Gabe?'

The question packed an unexpected punch; driving down deep to the part of himself he'd protected with barriers after she'd left him and then locked down tight after the debacle with Jenna. *Do you love her?* It was the question he'd asked himself on Saturday and hadn't been able to answer.

'Elly, you're my best friend, my lover, and in my eyes the mother of my children.'

'Your children.' She bit her lip, her teeth white against the plump crimson of her lipstick. 'But not *our* children.'

'Of course they're *our* children.' He tried not to shout because he really needed her to understand

and right now the argument was going round and round in circles. He wanted to hold her, stroke her hair, tell her it would work out for the best his way, but every part of her vibrated with rigid tension.

He dragged in a breath. 'A wise woman once told me I needed to honour Jenna through the children and that was the way to move forward. You, me and the kids, we're a family and that's moving forward.'

She sighed, the long, resigned sound circling him. 'I no longer want to be the convenient choice to help you absolve your guilt about Jenna.'

'Don't be ridiculous.' His words shot out hot and indignant. 'You are not a convenient choice!'

She raised her chestnut brows in a questioning arch. 'I think I am. I was willing to wait, Gabe. I wanted to trust and believe that you would change your mind about our baby but this time I'm not misunderstanding anything at all, am I? This time there is no maybe; your decision is an absolute and final no, and that means I can't marry you.'

Fear coalesced into anger. 'You're going to

walk away from a ready-made family because you can't have a child of your own?' His fist hit the table, making the cutlery jump. 'And here I was thinking that the selfish princess had grown up. Perhaps it *is* better we don't get married because the triplets don't need the experience of one child being favoured over them.'

Her gasp slapped him and he tried not to care. She was the one rejecting him. Again. 'I suppose it was a crazy idea to think you might have changed and that you would love my children enough to stay.'

'And I was crazy enough to think you loved me.'

He threw out his arms. 'What I'm offering you is better than love but you're too self-obsessed to see it!'

Her chair scraped across the floor as she shot to her feet, doubling over for a moment before she stood tall and straight. 'Goodbye, Gabe.'

He watched her go in a haze of *déjà vu*, letting her walk away from him as he simmered in anger, rejection and bitter disappointment. He'd been a fool to think that the triplets would be enough for her and that she'd stay so together they could make it work. He'd been a total and utter fool.

CHAPTER ELEVEN

ELLY sat down at the nurses' station, looked at the clock and dropped her head onto the desk. How could it only be one o'clock? The rest of the afternoon stretched ahead of her and her receptionist had already texted to tell her the clinic was fully booked.

She'd dragged herself out of bed again that morning and for the second day in a row she felt listless and exhausted, but she guessed that walking away from the man and children you loved would do that to a woman. She'd spent the last two nights staring at the ceiling, unable to sleep and not even able to toss and turn, because moving quickly caused the strained ligament to catch, sending red-hot pain through her. Gabe had joked it was a hernia and although she was certain it was nothing more than a strain, it was taking its own sweet time to improve.

Part of her welcomed the physical pain because it took her mind off the black hole inside her; a hole that alternated between sizzling with anger and pain, and aching with emptiness. Either way it was a constant companion of grief. She still found it hard to believe that her dream had shattered so quickly and so irrevocably that it now lay in jagged shards around her heart. Her head danced a continuous tango of 'How could you have let yourself love him again when he hurt you so much last time' with 'I never stopped loving him and I truly thought he loved me'. And that was the biggest kicker of all. Gabe didn't love her.

Her throat tightened as it always did when she let her thoughts go to that soul-destroying place. He wanted her in his life but not what she wanted in her life, and today he and the triplets would leave Midden Cove and head back to their life in Melbourne. Next week she'd have to politely enquire about them when she bumped into Cathleen and James at Coast-Care or in town. Dear God, she didn't think she could do that.

Tears pricked the back of her eyes and she

blinked rapidly to keep them at bay. She would *not* break down at work. She saved her meltdowns for the sanctuary of home and that wasn't going to happen for at least six hours.

'Elly, what are you doing?'

She slowly raised her head to see Sarah—who'd just arrived for the afternoon shift—leaning against the desk. 'I'm just taking a speed rest before I go into action.'

Sarah frowned. 'Have you seen yourself in the mirror lately?'

'I have, and I think these massive black rings under my eyes make me look extremely alluring.' She sat up, stretched and immediately winced as the pain in her lower abdomen caught her again.

'You're not coming down with the bug half the town has, are you? Fever, vomiting?' Sarah reached out her hand, resting it on Elly's forehead. 'You seem a bit hot to me.'

She shook her head. 'We're all hot today, just like yesterday. Johnno assures me that the missing part for the air-conditioning arrived in Devonport this morning and is on its way down here now.'

'That's good but, still, your eyes look a bit glassy. Are you sure you're not coming down with something?'

Elly bit her lip, knowing that the unshed tears were the culprits for her glazed-eyed look but she wasn't up to telling Sarah anything just yet, especially in the middle of A and E, but she threw her friend a bone. 'I took your advice and dumped Dev.'

Sarah rolled her eyes. 'I worked that out a couple of weeks ago but dumping Dev should have you glowing, not looking like death. So spill. If you're not coming down with something, what is it?'

'Elly.' Sandy hurried over. 'Gerald Ferguson's arrived with chest pain. I've given him oxygen, attached him to the ECG and drawn blood for enzymes.'

As Elly turned her head toward Sandy, Sarah whispered into her ear, 'You're not off the hook, you know. I expect to hear everything later.'

Elly gave a weary nod and rose slowly to her feet to avoid aggravating the pain, which now seemed to have moved to her groin. She accepted the ECG tracing from the other nurse, staring at it and seeing the unwelcome ST elevation. 'You're an absolute star, Sandy. I better go and administer some meds.'

Gabe stared at the pile of travel bags, all zipped up and waiting to be loaded into the car. Thankfully, this time tomorrow he'd be back in his apartment and in a thriving city of four million people where, unlike Midden Cove, he could be invisible if he chose. Midden Cove was too small and it had contracted even further now he was avoiding running into Elly. Neither of them needed that because after the other night there was nothing left to say.

He couldn't wait to get back to throw himself into work and throw all thoughts of Elly's betrayal out of his heart. Being back in Melbourne was the key to him moving on because while he was in Midden Cove everything reminded him of Elly and he woke up each morning to feeling angry desolation that she wasn't next to him and that she didn't want what he'd offered.

You didn't offer her love.

Love only causes anguish and despair.

He'd offered her something better; his children and his deep and abiding affection.

His father had taken the triplets out into the garden, leaving him free to pack, and now the job was done he wandered into the kitchen.

Cathleen turned from the sink. 'All packed?'

'All packed.' He picked up the kettle and checked for water, and on finding it full he switched it on. 'It's a late sailing so we can spend the morning at the beach and they can have a nap before we head north.'

'That's a sensible plan.' She grabbed some oven mitts and pulled two hot baking trays out of the oven. 'I thought I'd send you on your way with some chocolate-chip cookies. They're the triplets' favourite.'

'What about me?' He plucked one off the tray, tossing the hot biscuit between his fingers. 'They're my favourite too.'

She laughed. 'I remember. They were the only thing you were ever interested in cooking.'

'They're *still* the only thing I'm interested in cooking. I pay a woman to come in once a week and she cooks and freezes all our meals—that way I know we're eating healthily.'

His mother expertly slid the cookies onto the cooling racks. 'We all have our strengths, darling, and domesticity was never one of yours, but you've surprised us all with the marvellous job you're doing with the children. Sole parenting is never easy.'

Old irritation resurfaced as the kettle pinged and shut off. 'I don't really have much of a choice, do I?'

'We all have choices.' Cathleen frowned. 'I know the triplets were completely unplanned and that life with Jenna was difficult, but you don't have to raise them on your own for ever. You'll meet someone who loves you and the triplets, and wants to be part of your life.'

'You think?' He poured boiling water over the fragrant tea leaves in his mother's white china teapot and his hurt and anger poured out with it. 'Maybe I asked the wrong woman, then, because Elly doesn't want us.'

The oven tray Cathleen was holding clattered onto the sink. 'You asked Elly to live with you? But I thought you said it was all about the sex?'

'Damn it, Mum, I'm thirty-five years old and it's not right for us to be discussing my sex life.' He tugged the tea cosy hard over the pot and ground his teeth. 'And to set the record straight, what I actually said was that we were friends and you told me not to confuse friendship and sex.'

'And did you?' Eyes very similar to his own held his gaze with unstinting frankness.

No! He hauled open the fridge and grabbed the milk. 'Elly and I are great friends. We get along really well most of the time and she's great with the triplets so I thought we'd be good together, that we'd make a solid team to raise the triplets.'

'Ah.' She dumped the cooking implements into the sink.

'What the hell is that supposed to mean?'

'It sounds like you offered her a business agreement.'

Do you love me, Gabe? He slopped tea into two mugs, his hand gripping the teapot so hard it cramped. 'It was so much more than that! It was a future, a life together, her opportunity for the triplets to be the children she'd always wanted. It should have been a win-win situation, but she threw it all back in my face because she doesn't want us, she just wants a child of her own.'

Cathleen stared at him, her expression disbelieving. 'But I've seen the affection Elly has for the triplets.'

'Yeah, well, it's not enough for her.' His bitterness scalded his throat along with the hot tea.

Cathleen gave him a pitying look. 'Of course it isn't enough. Elly will want to make her new family complete by having a child with the man she loves.'

God, what was it with women? Why couldn't they be rational? 'But that's the point, Mum. With Elly we're complete the way we are, and she has a strong line of twins in her family. I can't parent more children. Half the time I'm drowning with the three I've got.'

'Do you love her, Gabriel?'

He ploughed his hand through his hair as the quietly-spoken words sliced through him. 'Elly and I were together for a year of euphoric highs and gut-wrenching lows that sent us spinning into an emotional maelstrom we couldn't navigate ourselves out of. When we split I met Jenna, and you know how that turned out. Love wasn't even in the picture, and by the end of that nightmare I struggled to even find affection.'

He blew out a long breath. 'If what Elly and I had back in Melbourne was love, then I can't do it. Not again. But I can do what we've had in the last few weeks. It was less fraught, it brought us together and it was…' He struggled to find the word. 'It sounds ridiculous but it was peaceful.'

Cathleen sipped her tea. 'That's love too, Gabe.'

He shook his head emphatically, shutting out the words. 'It's a brand of friendship.'

She responded in kind and put down her mug. 'Love changes over time. When I met your father it was all high excitement and high drama and we fought hard and made up even harder. There were times when we almost separated but we knew we belonged together too much, and thankfully we recognised that love comes in different guises. It changed and became a caring and companionable togetherness but that doesn't mean the high-octane passion goes, it's just expressed differently.'

She tilted her head in a knowing look. 'Seeing I'm not allowed to discuss your sex life, I'll leave you to work out what I mean. But let me tell you one last thing—if you wake up in the morning and feel lost without Elly, then you love her, no matter what names you want to give to those feelings.'

He thought of how much he missed her in his bed, of how his arms ached to hold her and how much he craved their long conversations and laughter. But then the anger and hurt swirled inside him, biting and scratching, reminding him of the pain they caused each other, and he drained his tea. 'Thanks for the kitchen philosophising, Mum, but Elly and I aren't you and Dad. It's over.'

Gerald Henderson's arrival was just the start and Elly hadn't actually made it back to the clinic due to the flux of emergency cases. So far she'd administered a Ventolin nebuliser for

Tommy Argenti's asthma, insulin for a tourist's hyperglycaemia, removed a fish hook that had become deeply embedded in an amateur fisherman's thumb and she was now stitching up Josh Reardon's palm after he'd disagreed with a knife.

'Right, Josh, you need to keep that clean and dry for five days but even after that don't go dragging it in the dirt. Make an appointment to see my practice nurse for removal of the stitches in about nine days.'

'Don't worry, Elly, I'll make sure he's good.' Sally turned to her husband, who was looking pale and slightly green after seeing blood gush out of the deep wound. 'Come on, honey. I'll tuck you up on the couch with the remote.'

As Elly peeled off her gloves, she wished she could lie down, close her eyes and tuck up in bed. Her head pounded and she hoped that the now-fixed air-conditioning would hurry up and start cooling the hospital down because she felt very hot. She grabbed a glass of water before heading back to check on Gerald Henderson, savouring the coolness as it slipped down her throat.

Gerald, a burly farmer, sat propped up against a pile of pillows with oxygen prongs in his nose, an IV dripping into his arm and the leads of the monitor keeping him firmly in bed. His bulk dwarfed the hospital's narrow bed, making him look out of place, but the fear in his eyes told her he was most definitely a patient.

Sarah pressed a button on the IV pump and threw Elly a worried look.

Elly caught the look and was surprised because she thought her patient was looking a lot better than he had an hour ago. She reached for the chart and red-hot pain tore down her leg, forcing her to grip the bed-end. She tensed and the pain intensified so she blew out a long, deep breath and the spasm passed. Elly managed to pick up the chart and decided the first spare moment she had she'd ultrasound her groin to see if she'd done some real damage to herself. And she vowed she was never lifting heavy boxes again. 'How's the pain now, Gerry?'

'I think I'm doing better than you, Doc. You don't look so good.' The farmer's sun-lined face creased in concern.

Elly tried to smile. 'Don't worry about me. It's nothing a good sleep won't fix.' *Sleep doesn't mend a broken heart.* She flicked through the chart. 'Now, I need you to tell Sarah if the pain changes in any way, OK? This is not a time to be stoic, Gerry, because we need to monitor your heart and keep it as healthy as we can.'

The farmer nodded, his expression resigned. 'Righto. Listen, seeing as I'm here, would you mind looking at a spot on my back? The wife's been nagging me to come and see you.'

'Of course. Happy to.' Elly moved in closer to the bed and slid one arm under Gerry's while Sarah did the same on the other side. 'On the count of three lean forward, Gerry. One, two, three.'

Elly pulled as Gerry leaned and pain exploded. Searing, burning, tearing pain, ripping through her from her groin to her shoulder. She pitched forward, her legs unable to hold her as her vision blurred and bile spilled into her throat.

'Elly!'

'Doc!'

She tried to speak but she couldn't move air

in or out of her lungs as the pain shattered her, leaving no part of her unscarred. She wanted to curl up, stretch out, do something, anything to make the pain go, but it gripped her like a vice, stealing everything from her.

She felt Sarah's hands on her, easing her off Gerry and moving her onto the floor. She immediately rolled onto her side, pulling her legs up to her chin, trying to banish the pain. She heard the rip of Velcro and the touch of the blood-pressure cuff and then Sarah's voice, sounding like it was coming from a long way away.

'Elly, where does it hurt?'

She tried to say, 'Here' but she couldn't. Her hands gripped her stomach as her head spun and blackness swirled at the edges of her mind.

'Elly, stay with me. I'm putting in an IV.'

She vaguely heard voices shouting, feet running, but the pain dominated every single second, never lessening its grip. The darkness beckoned her, promising relief. She tried to fight it, tried so hard to concentrate on Sarah's voice, but the pain made her cry out and that made it triple in intensity. The temptation of the darkness became too much and she bargained. She'd just go there for a minute, just one minute to get some strength so she could cope, so she could survive.

'Elly, help's on its way.'

But she didn't want help. She just wanted the pain gone. The darkness enveloped her, washing over her like a velvet cloak. Peace at last.

Lucy climbed into the car first, settling into the middle car seat, and Gabe leaned over, clicking her in securely. On the other side of the car, his father lifted Rory into his seat and Gabe turned around and picked up Ben. Two minutes later all three triplets were securely ensconced and it was time to go.

Gabe turned to his mother. 'So, I'll see you in Melbourne in a month?'

She hugged him. 'Wouldn't miss it for anything.'

He hugged her back. 'Thanks for everything.'

His father walked around the car and extended his hand. 'Safe trip.'

'Thanks, Dad.' He returned the handshake and

then hugged his father and gave him a short slap on the back.

'Oh, is that the phone?' His mother tilted her head toward the house as the faint sound of a bell drifted out on the afternoon air.

'Let it go to the message bank and we'll catch up later.' James waved to the toddlers, blowing kisses.

Gabe opened the driver's seat door and felt his phone vibrate in his pocket. As he pulled it out, the whoop-whoop of a police siren screamed across the summer air, immediately followed by the ear-splitting sound of the Tasmanian Fire Service's alarm. Was it fire practice?

He brought the phone to one ear and put a finger in the other so he could try and hear. 'Gabe Lewis.'

'Gabe, it's Sarah. Elly's sick, she's passed out.'

'Did she faint?'

'No, Gabe, it's serious.' The usually happy nurse sounded distraught. 'She's collapsed.'

The unexpected words penetrated, sending

terror tearing through him, fuzzing his brain and scaring the hell out him. 'Where are you?'

'At the hospital.'

The police car pulled up behind his, the siren silenced, and the sergeant got out, beckoning Gabe with frantic hand signals.

'I'm on my way. Stay on the line.' He threw his car keys to his father. 'It's Elly. I have to go to the hospital. Please look after the kids.'

Without waiting for confirmation, he ran to the police car, nodding his thanks to the police officer, all the time with his phone pressed to his ear, trying to find the doctor deep down, beyond the fear. The police car reversed with a squeal of tyres and a screaming siren as Gabe pulled his seat belt into place.

'Sarah, what are her vitals?'

'She's hypotensive and tachycardic.'

This isn't good. 'Run in a litre of Hartmann's. Is she in pain?'

'She's mostly unconscious.' Sarah's voice rose in a wail. 'I've called the air ambulance for evacuation but, Gabe, I'm really scared.'

Dear God, so was he. People didn't just collapse

and this wasn't Melbourne Central with its high-tech A and E and a suite of operating rooms at the ready. 'I'm two minutes away, Sarah.'

It was the longest two minutes of his life. He ran into A and E and Sandy, her face alarmed, grabbed his arm.

'She collapsed with a patient and we've got her on a monitored bed.'

Together they ran up the main corridor and into a two-bed bay. A curtain had been pulled between the beds but nothing prepared him for what he saw. His amazing, vibrant Elly lay moaning in coma position, her face whiter than the sheets she lay on with the exception of fire-engine-red cheeks. A large fan blew air across her as an IV pumped in fluid. Her blood pressure displayed on the monitor along with her rapid heartbeat showing how desperately ill she was.

He wanted to throw himself at her, hold her tightly and never let her go, but he had to be the doctor.

'Oh, thank God.' Sarah greeted him. 'She's pyretic with a fever of forty-one Celsius and she's in so much pain.'

He grabbed a stethoscope. 'Give her oxygen and ten milligrams of morphine along with IV paracetamol.' He squatted down so his head was at the same height as hers. 'Elly, sweetheart, it's me, Gabe.' He touched her arm and her eyes flickered open for a moment and stared at him unfocused and vacant. 'Elly, can you hear me?'

But she didn't speak and her eyes fluttered closed.

Panic morphed from simmer to full boil. He rolled her onto her back and palpated her abdomen. It was like pressing into solid wood. He listened for bowel sounds but there were none, and with her symptoms, septic shock was a big possibility. He'd stake his life on peritonitis but he had no clue to the cause, which could be any number of things from a ruptured appendix to a bowel obstruction.

An ultrasound would tell him but knowing wouldn't solve anything because Elly needed surgery. Now. But he wasn't a surgeon and even if he was, Midden Cove didn't have an anaesthetist. They might only be a short flight from Hobart but it might as well be a million miles when she needed intervention ten minutes ago.

Ectopic pregnancy. The thought rocked through him so hard that he found it difficult to breathe. *No, they'd used contraception.* But the doctor in him knew even in the most skilled hands, contraception could fail.

Elly and his baby.

Their child.

His heart cramped and a cry strangled in his tight throat. God, how selfish had he been to think he didn't want another child; his and Elly's.

The monitor started beeping wildly as Elly's pulse tore up to dangerous levels. 'I'm starting her on broad-spectrum antibiotics.' He pulled open the drug cart, his fingers fumbling with the vials. He was an emergency physician but even with all his experience and expertise he was virtually impotent to save the woman he loved.

I love her.

He waited for the gasping shock, the pain that always came when he'd thought about loving her in the past, but it didn't come. What came instead was soul-destroying reality; the vivid pitch-black image of what his life would be without her in it.

God, he'd been such a bloody idiot. A fool of the first degree.

'How long until the air ambulance arrives?'

'I'll check the ETA.' Sandy ran for a phone.

The monitor beeped insistently. 'Pressure's dropping, Gabe.'

She could die.

No! He wouldn't let her; he'd move heaven and earth to keep her alive. Elly was the missing piece of himself and he'd fight to the death to have the chance to tell her how much he loved her. He'd show her how wrong he'd been, try to make it up to her and somehow redeem himself in her eyes, even if she never wanted to have anything to do with him again. He ripped open a cannula and tightened a tourniquet around her arm. 'We need plasma expander and where the hell is that helicopter?'

An air-horn blasted outside.

'It's here.' Sandy raced back in, quick releasing the wheel brakes so they could manoeuvre the bed to the ambulance bay.

As he prepared to evacuate, Gabe leaned down and kissed Elly's fire-hot forehead. 'I love you, El. I know I don't deserve you, but keep fighting, sweetheart. Please. Keep fighting.'

CHAPTER TWELVE

ELLY opened her eyes to flowers. More flowers than one person deserved, and they covered the small shelf designed for such arrangements, her bedside table, her over-bed table, and three baskets were on the floor. It seemed every time she closed her eyes for a nap, more arrived. She picked up some cards and tried reading them but when she saw James and Cathleen's names on the fourth one, the rest slipped from her fingers. She stared out the ward window, hoping to see something, anything that would empty her mind of anyone with the surname Lewis.

Bright blue sky shimmered through the glass and that was all she could see from her third-floor bed. She turned away because the colour instantly reminded her of Gabe's eyes. Why did the Lewis family seem to surround her when she wanted only to forget?

Gabe was with you. She had vague memories of Gabe last night, calling out orders and holding her hand in the helicopter, but she hadn't seen him this morning because he'd probably returned to Midden Cove and the triplets. *Or Melbourne.*

But she refused to think about that.

She had, however, seen the surgeon who operated on her last night and his bland and uncompromising words had scarred her heart with thick pockmarks that would never fade. He'd saved her life but at what cost? But she didn't want to think about that either so she closed her eyes and retreated to the fuzzy post-anaesthetic place that let her sleep and pretend everything she held dear hadn't been stolen from her.

She heard footsteps and opened one eye to see a nurse checking her IV.

'How are you doing?' The nurse, whose name badge said 'Carolyn', had a caring smile and she pulled up a chair. 'It's a lot to process, isn't it? If you have any more questions we can get Mr Ross back to explain it again. You just say the word.'

The thought of hearing the surgeon's sonorous voice issuing his brutal verdict again was more than she could bear. 'I don't think that will be necessary.'

'OK, but if you change your mind just ask. Meanwhile, I have a message for you.' She pulled a note out of her pocket. 'Sarah says you're never to scare her like that again and you're not to worry about anything because they've got a doctor and everything's under control.'

Elly wondered who. 'Is it Dr Lewis?'

'No, because I'm here.'

Gabe's deep, rich voice filled the room and he strode in, wearing the royal-blue shirt that always made him look indecently handsome. A shirt that made her knees go weak and one she'd pulled off him in a frenzy of lust every time he'd worn it.

The memory sent a streak of longing through her and her heart hiccoughed, but she hardened it with steel. *He doesn't love you, remember.*

Carolyn gave him a winning smile. 'Good to see you again, Gabe.'

Gabe?

Carolyn stood up. 'Did you get that information you were after?'

He returned her smile and waved a tube of

papers scrolled up with an elastic band. 'I did. Thanks so much for your help.'

'No problem.' She turned back to Elly and adjusted the buzzer. 'Ring if you need anything and I'll be back in a bit with your antibiotics.'

Part of Elly wanted the nurse to stay but the other part wanted to get Gabe's obligatory visit and farewell out of the way.

He sat down next to her, the lines around his eyes even deeper than they'd been when he'd first arrived in Midden Cove. He banged the scroll of papers on his knee in a nervous tattoo. 'Hey.'

'Hey.'

Strained silence circled them, reminding her of how much things had changed between them.

'Where are the trip—?'

'How are you feel—?'

They spoke at the same time, their words colliding, tight with tension.

She had no energy to do this. 'You go first.'

He looked unsure but a moment later said, 'The triplets are with Mum and Dad so they're fine and the spoiling continues a little longer. But it's you I'm worried about. Hell, Elly, you gave us a fright.'

'Sorry.' She had no idea why she was apologising but he looked so bereft that it had just slipped out. 'I thought I'd just pulled a muscle or strained a ligament.'

He looked at her in wonder. 'You must have an unbelievable pain threshold.'

She felt tears prickling her eyes but she refused to cry in front of him. 'I wish I hadn't. If I'd done something earlier I might still…' She stopped speaking as her voice started to wobble and she could feel herself losing control.

He picked up her hand and gave it a squeeze. 'Shh, it's OK.'

She stared at him incredulously. 'I'm not one of the triplets, Gabe. I can't be consoled with a bit of a pat and a "there, there". It's not OK. It's so, so far from being OK but of course you'd think that!' Her chest tightened, her throat started to close and she tugged her hand out of his. 'I don't understand why you're here. Thank you for everything you did last night but you're off the hook, Gabe. You're free to leave and go back to Melbourne.'

His face blanched and abject sadness crawled through his eyes. 'Elly, I'm sorry, that's not what I meant at all. Of course what happened is not OK but…' He ran his hand through his hair. 'God, I'm making a complete hash of this so I'll just say it. I love you, Elly.' His voice dropped even deeper. 'I've been a complete moron and I'm so sorry it took almost losing you to make me realise that I've always loved you.'

She stared at him completely speechless and he kept talking as if now he'd started he couldn't stop.

'But the love I feel for you now is so very different from what I felt when I first met you that I didn't recognise it as love. I'm sorry, I should have known because this love, Elly, it's bone deep. It's as much a part of me as my own skin.'

Her head pounded, her belly ached and his words fell like heavy stones against her battered and bruised heart. 'You love me?' She couldn't hide the incredulity in her voice.

He leaned in close, his eyes filled with adoration

and a goofy smile on his lips. 'I love you. You're my soul mate, my missing half, and life without you would be too hard to contemplate.'

Her heart lurched in her chest but she clamped down on it hard. Gabe was saying everything she'd longed to hear and more, but today it was far too easy for him to confess to loving her. 'Isn't this declaration just a bit too convenient?'

His expression became wary. 'I don't understand.'

Her fingers fiddled with the top sheet. 'You love me now, today; the day I found out that I've lost an ovary and a fallopian tube to a chocolate cyst, and my other tube is so badly scarred with adhesions from having undiagnosed endometriosis that I'm technically infertile. You know that, right?'

He nodded wordlessly.

Her heart twisted in her chest and she wanted so badly to hurt him like she was hurting. She wanted to send him away and a bitter laugh exploded from her throat. 'The man who doesn't want any more children just got a gift.'

But he didn't push his chair back and storm

out. Instead, he sat perfectly still, silently staring at her as if he couldn't get his fill. Then he laid his hands on the bed, palms up. 'I deserved that. You're right, I was so wrong and I'm desperately sorry. I was selfish and so caught up in how us having children would impact on me I couldn't see your point of view at all. But I get it now. You're right, our child would complete our family and you deserve to have our child. I want us to have that experience.'

Somehow she held herself together. 'It's all a bit late, Gabe, and they're easy words to speak when the chance of me getting pregnant now is so remote.'

He unrolled the sheaf of papers from his pocket and she caught the logo of Melbourne IVF. 'Elly, if you'll forgive me, take me back and marry me, then as soon as you're fit again I'll do everything I can, explore every option we have to get us pregnant with our baby.'

Her gaze flickered between the information sheets and his face, as her fuzzy brain tried to work out what this all meant. Could she really believe him? Finally, she rested her gaze on him, forcing herself to really look at him, but not through her veil of hurt but with new and fresh eyes. She saw vivid blue depths filled with remorse, contrition, hope and love.

He loves you.

This is him showing you how much he loves you.

He was offering her IVF, which was not an easy road to travel and came with no promises and a likelihood of heartache. Oh, my God, he really did love her. He *had been* speaking the truth when he'd said he wanted her to have their child, the one she'd longed to have for so long.

She ran her finger across the words *in vitro fertilisation* and took in a deep breath. 'You realise that twins are a very strong possibility with IVF.'

'So we'll buy a people mover and a big house in a leafy suburb.' He shrugged. 'If we have twins there's a certain rightness to that because before this all happened you probably would have had them anyway.'

She bit her lip against the wave of happiness that was swelling inside her despite herself, and she fought to ask the hard questions. 'Gabe, this means hormone injections, me probably being grumpy, uncertainty, heartache and you having to deposit semen in a jar.'

He grinned at her, his eyes bright, and he winked. 'Perhaps you can help with that.'

She laughed and immediately regretted it as pain from her surgery shot through her, but she didn't care. Gabe loved her. Gabe truly loved her.

He rested his head against hers. 'Elly, I love you more than I can say.'

She rested her palm against his stubbled cheek. 'I love you too, Gabe. You, Rory, Lucy and Ben, and I've been miserable without you.'

'So have I.' He tucked the unruly strands of hair behind her ear. 'Will you marry *me*?'

This time she heard the distinction, this time she heard the love. 'I will.'

He tilted her chin with his finger and gazed into her eyes. 'I promise you, El, I'll listen. Compromise can be our motto.'

He looked so earnest and his eyes glowed brightly with his love for her. She wanted to hold him close and hug him tight but her tender belly disagreed so she moved her mouth to his instead and kissed him, sealing herself to him for ever. And he kissed her back.

EPILOGUE

SUMMER holidays meant long, lazy days at Midden Cove for the Lewis family, and this year was no exception. Elly finished setting the long table in preparation for the feast that James and Cathleen were preparing in her kitchen, and then she stepped outside and rang the old ship's bell on the large deck.

Gazing out toward the beach, she smiled as she watched Gabe and the children make their way back to the house. The triplets, now six, raced up the dunes lead by Rory with Lucy fast on his heels. Ben happily strolled behind his siblings and Gabe followed with Katie on his shoulders. As he reached the top of the dune he stopped and waved, a broad smile splitting his handsome face.

Her heart rolled over and she waved back, loving the man and marvelling that with every passing year it was possible to love him even more. His face wore a few more lines on it than it had five years ago but that only made him even sexier than before in a rugged kind of way. They'd weathered some tough times but they'd done it together and Katie was an unexpected and special gift they'd almost given up on.

'Mum, Ben found a seal ribcage on the beach and it still had some of its skin!' Rory panted out the news as his sandy feet hit the bottom step of the deck.

Elly smiled at the fact that the more gruesome something was, the more it impressed the boys. 'Awesome.' She put her hands on her son's shoulders and headed him back down to the outside shower to de-sand.

'And Katie kept sitting on our sandcastles.' Lucy shivered as the cold water tumbled over her.

'Just like you did when you were fifteen months old.' Gabe leaned in close to Elly, his eyes sparkling with love and banked heat. He kissed her on the forehead before transferring their toddler from his arms to hers.

'Did I?'

Gabe and Elly laughed at Lucy's angelic expression.

'You used to try and steal your brothers' ice creams.'

'Why do you and Dad always say things at the same time?' Ben gave them a curious glance.

Gabe slid his arm around her waist. 'Because when you love someone you often think similar thoughts.'

'Mum didn't think the same about the new boat. She said we didn't need it.' Rory dried his feet and dropped the towel.

Gabe looked sheepish. 'But we convinced her.'

Elly elbowed him. 'More like railroaded but that's OK. I have plans for a new bathroom here which seems like a fair-exchange.'

'Kids, dinner's ready!' James leaned over the deck and lifted Katie up into his arms as the triplets belted up the stairs.

'Be there in a sec, Dad.' Gabe grabbed her hand, and gently pulling her with him, walked around the corner to the front of the house and under the shade of the deck.

'What's going on?'

He stepped in close and she automatically leaned in, her body knowing exactly where to go so they fitted together perfectly.

'Mum and dad have offered to take the kids back to their place for a sleepover tonight.'

Elly smiled and a thrill zipped through her as she looked up into his eyes. 'Ah, so *that* would explain the look you gave me a moment ago.'

He grinned. 'What look?'

'The one that hopes you're going to get lucky tonight.'

He stroked her hair, his bluer-than-blue eyes sparkling with wicked intent and then he lowered his lips onto hers.

Tendrils of heat rocked through her and she sighed against his mouth, pressing into him, knowing absolutely that not only would he get lucky, she was the luckiest woman alive.

* * * * *

MEDICAL ROMANCE™

Large Print

Titles for the next six months...

September

SUMMER SEASIDE WEDDING	Abigail Gordon
REUNITED: A MIRACLE MARRIAGE	Judy Campbell
THE MAN WITH THE LOCKED AWAY HEART	Melanie Milburne
SOCIALITE...OR NURSE IN A MILLION?	Molly Evans
ST PIRAN'S: THE BROODING HEART SURGEON	Alison Roberts
PLAYBOY DOCTOR TO DOTING DAD	Sue MacKay

October

TAMING DR TEMPEST	Meredith Webber
THE DOCTOR AND THE DEBUTANTE	Anne Fraser
THE HONOURABLE MAVERICK	Alison Roberts
THE UNSUNG HERO	Alison Roberts
ST PIRAN'S: THE FIREMAN AND NURSE LOVEDAY	Kate Hardy
FROM BROODING BOSS TO ADORING DAD	Dianne Drake

November

HER LITTLE SECRET	Carol Marinelli
THE DOCTOR'S DAMSEL IN DISTRESS	Janice Lynn
THE TAMING OF DR ALEX DRAYCOTT	Joanna Neil
THE MAN BEHIND THE BADGE	Sharon Archer
ST PIRAN'S: TINY MIRACLE TWINS	Maggie Kingsley
MAVERICK IN THE ER	Jessica Matthews

MEDICAL ROMANCE™

Large Print

December

FLIRTING WITH THE SOCIETY DOCTOR	Janice Lynn
WHEN ONE NIGHT ISN'T ENOUGH	Wendy S. Marcus
MELTING THE ARGENTINE DOCTOR'S HEART	Meredith Webber
SMALL TOWN MARRIAGE MIRACLE	Jennifer Taylor
ST PIRAN'S: PRINCE ON THE CHILDREN'S WARD	Sarah Morgan
HARRY ST CLAIR: ROGUE OR DOCTOR?	Fiona McArthur

January

THE PLAYBOY OF HARLEY STREET	Anne Fraser
DOCTOR ON THE RED CARPET	Anne Fraser
JUST ONE LAST NIGHT…	Amy Andrews
SUDDENLY SINGLE SOPHIE	Leonie Knight
THE DOCTOR & THE RUNAWAY HEIRESS	Marion Lennox
THE SURGEON SHE NEVER FORGOT	Melanie Milburne

February

CAREER GIRL IN THE COUNTRY	Fiona Lowe
THE DOCTOR'S REASON TO STAY	Dianne Drake
WEDDING ON THE BABY WARD	Lucy Clark
SPECIAL CARE BABY MIRACLE	Lucy Clark
THE TORTURED REBEL	Alison Roberts
DATING DR DELICIOUS	Laura Iding

MILLS & BOON

WEB_M&B_RTL3 LP

Discover Pure Reading Pleasure with

Visit the Mills & Boon website for all the latest in romance

Buy all the latest releases, backlist and eBooks

Find out more about our authors and their books

Join our community and chat to authors and other readers

Free online reads from your favourite authors

Win with our fantastic online competitions

Sign up for our free monthly eNewsletter

Tell us what you think by signing up to our reader panel

Rate and review books with our star system

www.millsandboon.co.uk

 Follow us at twitter.com/millsandboonuk

 Become a fan at facebook.com/romancehq